MW01503812

PREYING MANTIS

Forgiving is not, forgetting...

Tanay Sawyer
434 Lime Grass Ave.
Las Vegas, NV 89183
725-231-3573
tanaycharea@hotmail.com

49,748 words

Dedication

This novel is dedicated to all my friends who have struggled or are struggling to rediscover themselves after a fall from a tumultuous relationship. Don't allow that piece of your past to define the who, you are tomorrow.

You can rise again, and you will.

3

CONTENTS

PREFACE

The inspiration for this novel stemmed from the struggle that our loved ones, family and friends have in relationships of all varieties. Some of us have a tumultuous relationship with ourselves and/or those around us, which inadvertently leads to behavior that is out of our character. Sometimes that behavior leads us down a dark path and it remains unseen until it's too late or we've hit rock bottom, hurting everyone we care about. But there's always an opportunity to make a choice. A choice to love ourselves. To forgive others. And to heal.

I want to acknowledge my mother, Deborah Lessane, for teaching me how to be a survivor, and my grandmother, Lois New, for showing me what love and adoration are supposed to feel like and how to shower others with the same care. That life-long encouragement, and the lessons imprinted on me helped transform me into who I am today.

6

Chapter 1
The Beginning

It's winter finals, and I don't know which is making me regret my life's decisions more, choosing architecture as my major or being the subject of Blithe's psychology paper. They're both pretty close. Staring at my half-finished blueprint for my fictitious high-rise, I hear Blithe mutter.

"Next question."

I spin my desk chair toward Blithe anticipating and hoping it will be her last question for the night.

"If love is a decision, how do you exp—." Blithe starts.

"*OH MY GAWD!*" I drop my head backward, staring blankly at the stained dorm room ceiling.

She chuckles. "I'm joking! But maybe it's not a bad idea to take a break."

I consider the benefit of allowing my brain to stop thinking on energy drinks. "I could probably take a nap."

Blithe snaps. "A *NAP*? Not really what I had in mind...*PIZZA!*"

I tilt my head to the side. "You just want to see your boy toy."

"Maybe, but you get pizza."

Cole and Blithe have been dating since sophomore year and they're still in the honeymoon phase. It's adorable, but it also makes you want to pop your eyes out like in Beetlejuice. There are only so many bunny nose kisses a person can see. But overall, he's a great guy.

My friends are the type who will push you off a cliff if it means better for you afterward. You might suffer a few bumps and bruises, but their intentions are always pure. Especially, Blithe. Since we randomly sat next to each other in English Literature for our first year at Boston University, we've 'real talked', cried, crammed, whined and laughed our way through. I taught her how to study, and she taught me how not to study so much. Balance. Although, her definition of balance also includes my love life. But with all my courses, I don't have the energy to devote to another person. Sounds like work, piled onto work.

***

Pizza does sound good, though. I lock the door and shuffle down the hall after Blithe, catching up just in time for a gust of frigid air to smack me in the face. My eyes widen and fill with tears, while my lungs gasp for another breath. *Do I really want pizza that bad?*

"Hurry up," Blithe calls from the middle of the campus walkway.

I jog toward her, and we speed walk to my car. A five-minute outdoor activity seems like an eternity in the bitter cold, until we hear the Greek sound of "Sigma Phi" being chanted by five frat bros passing a football. Blithe and I slowly come to a stop, staring at the middle of the courtyard, bewildered by the act.

"You guys are going to freeze to death," Blithe yells.

Her voice distracts as the thrower launches the football, and it's coming for us at full speed.

"*WATCH OUT!*" Blithe shouts as a human body propels me backward.

Then, I feel excruciating pain in my foot. I drop to the concrete like a cinderblock, howling for help that I know my peers can't offer. All the frat brothers gather around me as if they are being awarded their Greek letters, murmuring, "Is she ok? Should we take her inside?" Profanity spews from my mouth as I rest my chin on my bended knee, wrapping my mitten-covered hands around my shoe, hoping to help dull the pain.

"I'm so sorry!" one of the boys says. "I jumped up for the ball and came down on her foot."

"Come on, Franchesca. Can you get up and stand on it?" Blithe nurtures.

Two of the boys help lift me to my feet. I apply weight to the uninjured foot, then slowly guide my left foot forward for the pressure test. Placing it onto the ground, the piercing agony travels from the tip of my toe through my entire foot. As I wail for the pain to stop, my heart beats faster and I begin to sweat in the 35-degree weather. My body loses the strength to hold itself up and my mind transcends to darkness.

***

Beep… Beep… Beep… My sleep is interrupted, and I awaken to the smell of rubber gloves and plastic. I repeatedly lift my eyelids until my vision is no longer blurry. Catching a glimpse of the butterfly needle protruding from my arm, I snap into full consciousness, frantically shifting my eyes around the room for a semblance of familiarity. Trying to escape from my bed, not realizing a cast resting around my leg.

"Heeey! You're awake," exclaims a boy as he leaps from a cushioned hospital chair.

"Who are you? Where's Blithe?" I ask, taking in shallow breaths.

"No need to freak out. I'm Xander. The very apologetic guy that accidentally broke your foot."

"*MY FOOT IS BROKEN!?*"

Xander scratches his right temple. "Did the cast not give it away? I brought you flowers." He points to the vase of lilies.

"Oh great. Can you rub them on my cast? Maybe that'll heal me."

Exhaling deeply, he says, "I don't know what you want from me. I said I'm sorry, and I'm here."

***

I was left in the hospital for days, seeing that I had trouble learning how to function with crutches. But every day, Xander was there, pacing with me back and forth through the halls as I clumsily navigated my new wooden accessories. Encouraging me and evoking joy and laughter.

Blithe says, he is just what I need. Someone light-hearted to show me the other side of life.

On day three, I'm finally discharged with Xander by my side. It's nice to have someone show they care about me besides Cole and Blithe. Xander drives me home, walks me inside to my dim dorm room, only being illuminated by the shape-shifting wax of my lava lamp. He helps me across the room to my unkempt twin bed, but the best part is that it's against the only window in the room. I love to people-watch and see how nature transforms as time passes. It helps my mind escape reality, at least for awhile.

He sits on my bed. "So, what are you going to do now?"

"I don't know. Study. Look, these last few days have been great, and I thank you for all of your help, but you don't have to feel guilty anymore. I'm ok. You're off the hook. So, feel free to continue living your life as you normally would. Without me in it."

He chuckles. "I stopped feeling guilty after I apologized. I'm here because I want to be."

He stares at me with a crooked smile as I gaze at him blankly, trying to reach an itch inside my cast.

He grabs a ruler from my drawing table. "Here, let me help. Is the itch right here?"

I anticipate satisfaction. "A little to the left."

"Ahhhh." As I rest my head on the back of my neck.

He continues for a few moments before he replaces the ruler back to my desk.

"Thank you." I chuckle.

***

From that day on, Xander makes it his business to stop by my dorm room at least once a day to assess my healing as if he has just trained to be a medical assistant.

"Can you wiggle your toes? Remember not to put weight on your foot." He fills my room with aromatic florals and reminds me of the count down until the removal of my cast. I think he receives gratification from taking care of me.

Finally, the day of my cast removal arrives. I thank the heavens that I can move about on my own without restriction. Although, Xander seems to be concerned that it's too soon.

After the doctor removes the cast, he says, "Seems to have healed nicely," rotating my foot, while the nurse examines the x-rays.

"Hey doc. She still needs to stay off her foot even-though the cast is off, right?" Xander asks.

He glances at the nurse for confirmation. "Nope. She's all set to resume normal activities."

"YES"! As I jump out of bed, landing on both feet like a gymnast sticking their first landing.

I'm the most excited I've been in weeks. No more waddling around on arm stilts! No more being late for class from struggling to hop up two flights of stairs on one foot. My freedom has returned!

As we leave the hospital, I simulate tap dancing in my squeaky tennis shoes.

Snapping his head toward me. "You better knock it off before you break it again."

I continue to dance. "You heard the doctor. I can go back to doing what I want, but I won't be getting anywhere near you and a football." I chuckle.

"You're my girlfriend now, so I think my opinion matters."

I almost trip over my own feet at the sound of the word girlfriend. *I'm his girlfriend? When did this happen? Was I asleep? Because I don't remember consenting to this new role.* I haven't dated seriously while in college, so maybe this is the new way of courting. You want something, you go after it. Afterall, that's been my motto since my mother instilled it in me at age 12. It's not the worst thing that could slip from his lips. It is adorable of him to think he could have me, simply because he wants me.

"How long have you been thinking about this?"

He reaches for my fingertips. "Awhile," he says, gazing into my dark brown eyes.

"And you just made an executive decision without talking to me first?" I ask casually.

He releases my hand, forcing it back to my side. "I thought we were having a good time."

Resting my hand on his shoulder. "A good time doesn't mean girlfriend. Let me just think it over for a bit."

The car ride home is quiet. I sit in the passenger seat, watching my thumbs circle around each

11

other, while Xander uses his teeth to peel the skin of his bottom lip. I don't know if he is tense or just has dry lips. I don't know what to say, but I feel like I should say something. I look up from my thumbs, and we're parked in the student lot. I turn to him, my mouth slightly gaping for a peace offering, but he immediately swings the driver's door open and quickly escapes. I continue to sit as he walks toward the dorms.

Xander looks back. "Hey! Are you planning on sitting in there all night? I need to set the alarm."

I stare at him through the dirty windshield as he jingles his keys. Then I retreat from the vehicle. The alarm chirps as soon as my door closes. I sulk across the courtyard, my boots slowly crunching in the hardened snow. I watch him casually walk away until he disappears between buildings. The weight in my chest becomes heavier, like a dumbbell hanging from my neck and the pit of my stomach warms as I walk past the place where my broken foot began. This will now be a memory and I guess Xander will be too.

***

After a few days, I decide to call to clear the air. It rings a few times, then the voicemail chimes in. I'll try again tomorrow.

Tomorrow comes, and still nothing. I even try to text. I hate texting. Three days pass, and still no response, but I need to tell him what's on my mind. I want to know what was on his, even though it is seemingly evident by the unanswered communication. I attempt one last call in anticipation of his voicemail.

Hey Xander. It's Franchesca. I want to apologize if I hurt you with my response to your girlfriend comment. It wasn't you. I was surprised and didn't want to jump into anything before I had an opportunity to think about it. To think about everything. I understand if you don't want to see me again, but I need you to know that I appreciate everything you've done for me. I'll never forget it.

A few more days pass and still nothing. I haven't been rejected much in my life, but I'm not a fan. I've tried all that I'm willing to try. After all, I didn't know him that long. My life did come to a halt, classes didn't stop, nor did my heart break. So, farewell Xander. I sincerely wish you well.

It's the first weekend without my cast and I actually want to celebrate. I'm usually a recluse on

Valentine's Day, as I never have a date, but this year the lovers are going to have to share. The tough part will be finding a few friends to join in my fun. Needing to shower, I burst through our dorm room door, almost tripping over something colorful. Then, bringing myself to a halt on the tips of my toes, I take a peek at the obstruction at my feet.

"Oh my gawd. Blithe, come get these flowers. Cole left them in the most ridiculous place. I almost punted them across the hall."

She walks toward me with open arms ready to embrace the bouquet. They are beautiful. A teal opaque vase crowded with teal and white lilies. My favorite. They always illuminate the room with their floral sweetness.

"Cole is so sweet." She smiles.

"Open the card! Open the card!" I chant.

Blithe reads the card aloud...

Spending this day with you will make me a happy man. Honestly, spending any day with you. As I've gotten to know you, I realize that your personality lights a fire in my soul and your mind takes me on a journey. Allow me to pick you up this afternoon @ 3 for a Valentine's Day I hope you'll remember.

Happy Valentine's Day, Franchesca

- Xander

"*Xander?*" Blithe yells.

We shift our eyes toward each other as Blithe continues to hold the vase.

She peers into my soul. "What are you going to do?"

Hunching my shoulders, I say, "Thirty seconds ago, I was about to shower."

This is not how I thought my Saturday was going to be. Spending hours debating if I should go on a date with a guy who just spent the week ghosting me. Or weighing the possibility of him running off bleating like a baby goat if I say no. I thought I was free and clear from these types of decisions.

Blithe flails her arms. "Why don't you just go? At least you know where his head is.

I shift my eyes across the room. "I guess."

I spend hours laying on my bed debating if this decision should be as easy as blithe made it sound.

Could it be that simple?

Just go out with him, have fun and pick his frat-football brain. The closer to three o'clock it

13

becomes, the less time I have to cancel.

Moments pass as I drift into a meditative calm, until three consecutive knocks interrupt. My eyes shoot open, and my heart feels as though it might propel from my body.

Get up, Franchesca.

I slowly walk to the door with my arm extended, ready to twist the knob to reveal my expected guest. Pulling the door toward me, my breaths become shallow.

And forward steps a man I don't recognize.

Xander's former shoulder-length lochs have transformed into a short-hairs, barely an inch long. Short around the edges, but long enough on the top to run my fingers through. A forced part on the left makes him look cool, but distinguished. His wilderness beard no longer exists. No stubble. No scruff. No late evening shadow, only a visibly smooth, structured jawline leading to a crooked smile. My lids flutter in disbelief as my eyebrows reach for the ceiling.

Gliding his fingertips through his feather-like hair. "Are you ready to go?" He smiles.

I snap out of my visible stupor. "Right! Yes. We can leave."

We breach the dorm hall doors, and Xander guides me by the elbow as we walk between two buildings on campus. Hidden between them is the most beautiful picnic table my eyes have seen. Another bouquet of lilies stands in the middle of the table, shimmering in the sunlight. Beckoning me with its variations of pink and white coordination. As Xander and I draw closer, I see chocolate-covered fruit. Strawberries, pineapple and banana. *My favorite!* Four red mugs rest on each side of the table, waiting to be filled with non-alcoholic deliciousness. Xander planned folded blankets, propped candles, LED lighting wrapped around the table, extra gloves, and hors d'oeuvres. He has thought of everything. Even a pillow to soften the stiffness of the bench. He remembered everything I mentioned in casual conversation. Everything I like. All my favorite things.

"Wow! I don't know what to say."

"Say..." he ponders. "I'm hungry."

He smirks, raises one of the heated canisters, and begins pouring soup into one of the mugs. The aroma reminds me of my mothers' winter stew. That's what she calls it.

Chunks of potato, carrot, onion, celery, and beef pour into my cup.

"Did you make this?" Inhaling the herb-filled aroma.

"Yup. Just off campus in the frat boy kitchen."

14

We laugh as he pours himself a cup. I gently spoon the hot stew into my mouth, and it almost immediately warms my soul from the inside out. *Who knew this man had cooking skills?* Maybe Blithe is right. I should be more open to being open. There seems to be a lot more I could learn to like about Xander. After a few bites, he drops a handful of marshmallows in a nearby mug and begins to pour a steamy dark brown liquid over them. The white puffy pillows rise to the rim and he tops the mug with whipped cream.

Today, I decide to give Xander more than just awkward glances.

***

Weeks become months as the last snowfall begins to melt into the weathered lawn on campus. As Xander taps away on my laptop, I stare from my dorm room window, watching the trees sway before my thoughts begin to shift to the peace of mind I've acquired since being with him. Xander's tapping ceases, interrupting my thoughts, and before I realize how great our companionship has been, the phrase, "I love you," tenderly rolls through his lips. I stop my stride as we walk hand and hand through the campus courtyard. Curiously gazing into those deep brown eyes, ensuring I heard what I thought I did. As his delicate hand accompanies my face, he excavates my soul for loving reciprocity.

My heart flutters.

"I love you too."

For some reason, this moment feels different than all the others. Every time I've uttered these words to a man, I meant it, but with Xander, this moment is different. Time decelerates as his lips press against mine, and I lean into the fiery combustion inside my chest. I quickly begin to reevaluate my idea of what love is. *Did I ever really know what it was? Have I been loving with my head this entire time?* I feel like I'm finally using my heart for what it is meant to do. I'm *in love* with him.

He wraps his arms around me, and I make love for the first time in my life.

***

We spent months living in each-others company, 10 months to be exact. Blithe actually moved out of the dorm and in with Cole. This was always the plan for them as we approached our senior year.

Since we became exclusive, we haven't hung out with friends much. But recently, they've mentioned how they never see us anymore. So, we plan for a fun night at Dave & Buster's.

At this stage, Xander and I can effortlessly co-mingle in each-others friend groups, so when I see Mike, standing six feet tall, ordering a beer at the bar, I think nothing of approaching.

I place my elbow on his shoulder. "You mind getting me one of those." I chuckle.

"Ha ha, you're so funny. I don't supply underage college students with alcohol."

Glancing over my shoulder, I see Xander in the distance being a regular comedian with a few of his buddies, so I return my attention to Mike for a few more laughs. After some time, I decide to mingle with some others, but as I turn around, Xander becomes an instant obstruction. He startles me into almost dropping my milkshake. Firmly gripping my elbow, he guides me to a secluded area where he stares me in the face for seconds before allowing words to escape.

"Why were you flirting with Mike?"

Lowering my eyebrows. "Why would I be flirting with Mike?"

"I SAW you." trying not to raise his voice. "He bought you a milkshake, and you were all over him."

I deeply exhale. "First, why would we do that to you? Second, if we were up to no good, why would we do it in front of you? That's dumb."

"So, I'm dumb?" he demands, waiting impatiently for a response.

"No. What you're insinuating took place is dumb. Do you want me to stop hanging out with Mike?"

"You can be friends with who you want. Just *try* not to be all over them." He condescends.

Flailing my arms. "I wasn— Fine."

"I'm just going to go back to the frat tonight. Have fun with Mike." As he walks toward the exit.

"ARE YOU SERIOUS!" My voice travels across the open floor.

I refuse to leave our friends, as the whole point was to be with them tonight. As everyone begins to leave, I hitch a ride with Blithe, sparing no details of the earlier events, on the 20-minute ride back. She conjures a detailed diagnosis, but what I hear is that he may have some underlying issues to work through. It's our first fight. A minor speed bump on a long road to happiness and understanding. Blithe pulls into the parking lot of the dorms, and I immediately sprint out of the darkness into the well-lit corridor. Turning the key and entering my lava lamp-lit space, I glide to my bed and fall into it face-first. Then I hear a startling voice.

"I've been waiting for you all night," a voice asserts.

I screech, quickly lifting my body from the face-planted position to grab my lava lamp as a weapon.

"Whoa! It's me. Calm down."

My limbs quiver from terror. "Xander? I thought you were staying at the frat tonight?"

He's lying on the second bed, gazing up at the ceiling. "I decided to come home and wait for you, thinking you'd be here at a decent hour."

I look at the clock. "It's barely past midnight, and I don't have a curfew. Did you want to talk about something?"

He strides toward my bed. "No. I want to show you how much I love you. I get jealous because you're mine and I don't want other guys to get the wrong idea. You make me get jealous." He slowly unzips my coat.

Xander gives the gift of intermittent kisses on my lips, as I release each arm from my sleeves. I wrap my hands around his neck, pulling him closer.

"I love you too much for someone to take you away from me," he utters.

He buries his face into mine, and all is forgiven as we finish the night intertwined in each-others love.

***

The last several months of our relationship have been an emotional roller coaster. I no longer participate in social activities where his friends are present. Xander seems to think his friends and I are plotting romantic excursions whenever they're around. The previous time I waited for him at the frat house was my last. I was conversing with one of Xander's house mates in their living room, with whom I also have a class with. As we shared our thoughts on how emotional trauma can dictate ones' mentality and decision-making, Xander walked in, saw us sitting on the sofa, and immediately rushed over to accuse me of sitting too close to his friend. The final straw for Xander seemed to be my inability to continue to enable his behavior just to keep the peace.

A few weeks ago, he thought he had the authority to un-invite me to a mutual friend's birthday party because I had been to that specific venue with someone else. But, of course, I showed up anyway to celebrate with my friend, not Xander. There were laughing faces all around, until I locked eyes with

Xander. I continued conversing with my friends, anticipating his approach.

He leaned in. His lips pressed against my ear as he whispered the reminder of why I should be at home waiting for him. A fury grew inside my chest.

"WHO DO YOU THINK YOU ARE?!"

I spewed every offense he performed against me right back at him, while ensuring he knew exactly how insecure I knew he was. When my verbal assault was done, our friends in earshot greeted us again with raised eyebrows.

I constantly found myself in a battle between reality and his emotions. Somehow, he consistently manages to make me feel like his jealousy is a product of my actions. Though I continually search my mind for aimless flirtatious discrepancies, I'm unable to bring them to the surface, I don't know how to feel. This love I have is the first of its' kind. My heart bleeds at the anger in his eyes and the disappointment in his voice. With each event, he becomes more estranged, and I, more exhausted.

Going into my senior year, I decide to stay on campus for the summer. I opt to pile on a few more courses to take my mind off Xander, while he's in his hometown. After the last episode, he decided to break it off. Devastation is an under-statement. I begged and pleaded for five days, until he no longer answered my calls. I even stooped as low as to shadow his social media. I mourned this loss for months. But it's been a week since my last tear stained my pillow, and I'm beginning to function. Still broken, but functioning.

Trying to build the blocks I'll call my life, post-graduation, I plan to meet with the director, until a whiff of *his* cologne brings me to a halt while striding to her office. That sweet musk makes the hair on my arms rise. I quickly turn as if the scent had taken control of my body, closing my eyes. . .

"Franchesca," a voice calls.

My eyes startle open. "Hi." I quickly walk around him.

Xander gently wraps his finger around my wrist as I try to walk away.

"I've had a lot of time to think while I was away, and I realize I want you in my life. I want to build a life with you. Have you as the mother of my children."

I stand speechless. My heart thuds repeatedly as if it wants freedom from my chest. Happiness and confusion set in, but I don't care to understand. He reaches into his satchel and reveals a small, blue velvet box.

"Will you marry me, Franchesca?"

I feel the color drain from my face as disbelief travels through my mind like a pinball. *Can this really be happening?* My first love. My *only* love. The man I thought I'd lost forever, asking me to say yes to eternity. Xander opens the box and held in the middle is a single diamond shimmering in the sun from the nearby window. I drop my books to the floor.

"Yes. *Yes! YES*! I will marry you."

A smile graces his face, and he slides the diamond on my finger. Although, we've only been dating a year, you know when you know, right? And this feels perfect.

***

A few months have passed since the engagement, and we haven't given any time to a conversation about wedding planning. We've both been busy with finals, but now that they've gone, we can finally breathe. I regain excitement as I stare at the symbol of commitment on my finger and gleefully begin throwing out ideas for the wedding before Xander escapes the room again. Since finals ceased, he seems busier than I've ever seen. I know he's working on a big invention, but I have no idea what it is. All I know is I barely see him anymore, so I use the time I have with him wisely.

"Hey fiancé! Since we're both staying in Boston, I figured, we could start narrowing down some wedding venues."

"We have plenty of time for that. Graduation is in six months, and we don't have a date, anyway." He shrugs.

"So, let's pick a date," I exclaim.

He begins to rub my shoulders. "What's the rush? We'll figure it out." He kisses my neck as he walks back to the computer.

I reluctantly oblige. After all, we've been engaged for six months and haven't graced our parents with the news yet. But as month after month passes, I ask Xander the same question. "When should we tell our parents?"

He hasn't given me a date that I can look forward to. The most definite response I've gotten on the matter is, "Let's wait until after graduation." So, I take the initiative and spend weeks researching wedding essentials, so Blithe and I can go out and put our feet on the pavement. We sample local bakeries for the perfect cake, try on stunning bridesmaid dresses, and narrow pricing and availability on venues. She helps me with a down payment on Xander's wedding ring. This is the happiest time of my life. I never thought it would begin so perfectly.

We drive back to the dorms, so Blithe can help me organize all the information we gathered. I turn the key to my empty room and toss my keys on the bed. Xander is once again at the library. Wanting an excuse to see him on such a good day, Blithe accompanies me in surprising him with lunch from his favorite sandwich shop. She waits by the entrance as I walk the library isles, searching the tables for Xander. I squint but could see no one that resembles him. I try not to crumple the paper bag while walking through the book stacks. Finding no one, I retreat to the front desk.

"Have you seen Xander today?"

Jess shakes her head. "Not on my shift."

"Thanks." I nervously glide back to Blithe.

"What happened? He didn't want the sandwich?" Blithe inquires.

Smoothing my forehead with my index finger. I say, "He's not here. Hasn't been all day."

Blithe's eyebrows raise. "Oh."

We return to my room, and Xander is still absent. I swallow the lump sittings in my throat. I need to demand answers. I need to know why he isn't where he says he is. I sift through all the junk in my handbag to find my cell.

"What are you doing?" Blithe slowly walks toward me.

"I'M CALLING!"

Blithe quickly smacks the phone from my hand, and it lands across the room. "Don't do that. Calm down first. Maybe wait until you see him in person."

"I haven't seen Houdini in FOUR DAYS! I know he's been here. It just happens to be when I'm not."

"At least wait a day until you've calmed down and thought about what you want to say."

Here's mama Blithe with all her maturity. But I don't want to be mature right now. I want answers, but Blithe is ensuring I don't get any tonight.

***

The next morning Blithe and I wake up with no Xander. But that's typical these days. Then we hear fiddling with the door. I remove myself from the bed and open the door.

Xander stumbles inside. "I didn't know you'd be here. Sorry," he says, walking toward the second bed.

20

My eyes widen. "Sorry? Care to explain why you weren't at the library yesterday?"

He hesitates, quickly flashes a smirk and begins to walk toward me. He lifts my chin with his index finger, inching his face to me. Then intimately wrapping his lips around mine. The agitation in my chest begins to dissipate. I feel Blithe brush past me, and I hear the door close.

"I saw you and your paper bag." He chuckles. "I thought you were there to study, so I didn't want to distract you, and I also didn't want to be distracted," he says, offering me that crooked smile.

Maybe I did overreact. Maybe Jess just didn't see him in the library that day. Luckily, all the anger and anxiety begin to melt off of me.

Relief sets in.

Until I open the text image on my cell from my friend Alex. We've taken a few classes together and have become close over the past year. I tap the screen to open the message, and it's Xander bowling with a girl I don't recognize. I scroll to the next photo, and with both hands, he's clutching one of hers. My heart drops. I immediately show Xander the photo. He glances at it, but doesn't react. We share an unusual stare for what seems like a bi-millenary.

"Where did you get that?" he demands.

"It doesn't matter. Explain."

Flailing his arms. "She doesn't matter."

"Explain anyway," still holding up the photo.

He releases a long exhale. "She's my ex."

Quickly rising to my feet. "*The* ex? The one that broke your heart. The one you never want to talk about. The one that got away? *That* ex?"

"She came to town a few weeks ago and wanted to talk. I figured I'd give her the time of day."

"Give *her* the time of day?"

"You're my fiancé and I told her that. End of story." He glides toward me.

He strokes my hair as we face each other. His delicate hands calm my high temperature. I inhale deeply and gently exhale toward him. He always has a way to calm me down and reroute my mind. His gentle touch reminds me that his love for me will never waver, and soon he will be married to ME.

***

Finally, only a few weeks until graduation. I'm ecstatic! These last few months have been torture for me. Xander is still mostly missing in action. I'm wedding planning alone, finishing up my internship, and trying to study for finals. I just need a moment to exhale. Ready for a much-needed nap, I snuggle my favorite fleece blanket, but as my mind drifts, Xander storms in, aggressively removing each article of clothing as if they are soaked in acid. Without a word, he grabs his robe and shower caddy and swiftly exits the room. Shortly after he leaves, I hear *ding... ding.* I remove myself from the bed to find the location of the sound. *Ding... ding...* Patting down the second bed covered in Xander's clothes, I find the source in his pocket. Sliding the phone from his pant to toggle the notifications to silent when I notice all four alerts are from, Colleen. The former girlfriend. I want to replace the phone in his pocket. I don't want to be *that* girl. But I'm compelled to read them, so. I bring up the thread. ~ *I'm glad we had the opportunity to talk about everything, and I'm pleased we're on the same page. I'm sorry I wasn't strong enough for us to be together before.*

~ *Oh, by the way, I arranged to be in town so I can see you graduate!*

~ *My parents said hi! And they hope they can see you soon.*

~ *Can't wait for dinner tonight. I've been waiting to try this place all week. 7pm, right?*

My eyebrows raise in astonishment, and a warming sensation washes over me. *How much time does he need to give her? What does she think she's doing? Why didn't he tell me about this dinner?* I inhale deeply to prevent my thoughts from spiraling because I don't know how to handle this. Taking a moment to think calmly, I find a solution as I hear his voice permeate through the hall. Quickly replacing his cell, I jump into bed, pretending to be asleep as he opens the door. I hear Xander shuffle through hangers, seemingly trying to find the perfect outfit. As he softly closes the door, I smell a hint of the cologne he was wearing when he proposed.

My favorite.

I weigh the possibilities of what could be going on between them, with the reality of my trust in Xander. Nervously removing myself from the bed, I pace the room. I know my next move, but debating if it's a good one.

Screw it!

Wasting no more time, I jump in the car my parents bought me and speed out of the student lot. My hands tremble, while a whirlwind of confusing thoughts clouds my rationale.

22

As I approach my destination, I push a final breath from my lips before exiting my vehicle. My tennis shoes crackle on the newly paved asphalt as I make my way to the entrance. Tilting my baseball cap forward, I quickly scan the room and make a B-line for an empty seat at the bar.

Gotcha.

Using the selfie camera feature on my cell made it simple to watch from afar, even with the dim lighting. This phone made a lot of things simple, like sharing Xander's location. Looking through my camera, my anxiety is through the roof, but they seem platonically friendly. Just conversation with intermittent smiling and laughter. There's not even physical contact. I watch for a better part of 15 minutes; the most I've gotten out of this, is boredom.

But at least I know I was wrong. My world just turned itself right side up again. Before calling it quits, Xander removes himself from his chair. I assume he's on his way to the restroom, so I stay put. But, he reaches into his pocket, lowers himself to one knee, and presents a blue velvet box that holds the ring he offered me.

He said he was getting it cleaned.

Colleen jumps from her seat with genuine surprise. Tears of joy roll down her face, while tears of devastation stream down mine. I'm no longer viewing this "celebration" through the filter of a camera. I turn around to witness it with my own eyes. Standing paralyzed at the bar, phone in hand as Xander yells for a bottle of champagne.

I trusted him. I gave him all of me.

Removing my hat, not knowing what to do with my body, I see Xander acknowledge my presence. The joy evaporates from his face, and I stare back blankly, watching as he quickly offers money for the bill, leaving the restaurant, hand in hand with his new fiancé. The shattered pieces of my life fall away right before me, leading me on a trail to the only altar I'll ever see… graduation.

24

Chapter 2
Loveless Nights

THIS IS IT! This is my life. Four years out of college, a great architect filled with zero desire to be in a relationship with the male species. My heart is on its last life-line, and I have no intentions of reviving it. I promise if I fall in love again, I'll have myself committed. Why do people torture themselves with such nonsense?

Most people my age are in loving relationships, or even married, like my best friend Blithe. She's been married since graduation, and I thought that would be the future I'd have with my former fiancé, but he stole that from me. He stole everything. Who would ever think their first love would devour your human essence from the inside out? Destroying the fairytale of kismet spirits destined to be intertwined for eternity, while simultaneously altering my perception of relationships.

Luckily, I have Blithe consistently trying to keep me grounded. . . to little avail. These past few years, I've dragged her with me emotionally through endless semi-reckless behavior. I've been enjoying one-night excursions with men of my choosing, closing off anyone who mentions the idea of a relationship, which brings me to why I no longer go out with the same man twice. Gallivanting around town just to pick up guys for my personal wants is all I need.

And Blithe thinks its unhealthy. Now that she has her degree in Psychology, she likes to smack me in the face with it every chance she gets. It's comical and annoying at the same time, but I have my own ways of coping. I go out on "The Hunt," stalking my prey on late nights just to get an hour of satisfaction. Before morning, they're gone, and I can enjoy my coffee in peace.

This is my life. I have needs, but love isn't one of them.

Tonight, I'm in my favorite hunting ground. It's in a small section of the city that I like to call the party district. The entire stretch of road for five blocks is filled with bars, lounges, and dance clubs with a sprinkle of late-night eateries for the after-hour lushes. Martini Life is one of my favorites. It has red-painted brick exterior with two large bay windows flanking the entrance. Walking past, you can see the golden yellow sofas, plush throw pillows, and dimly lit chandelier fixtures. That's what made it easy for me to wander in to see more of the modernly rustic tapestries and décor.

As I walk inside, there's an aroma of potpourri. The type of smell that reminds you of the holidays. Almost like a pot of fresh cranberries, citrus, and cinnamon simmering on the stove! Not only is it a wonderland of comfort and pleasant smells, but there's also a sea of handsome men that brings a

26

smile to my face, something like the grinch!

Martini Life has become my favorite place to roam.

It's the start of my prowl, so I take my favorite seat at the counter with cushions that feel like padded air. Mm mm, so soft! Then, my face drops as I see who walks through the door.

"Blithe? What are you doing here?"

"It's Thursday night. Where else would you be?! I just stopped by to see how your weekend was going so far."

"It's early. I'm still checking out my prospects."

"How about that guy over there? He's handsome, tall, and has honey-colored eyes to die for."

"I've been watching him, and he spends too much time talking about himself. I wouldn't get one word in to invite him over to my place. Plus, I couldn't pretend to enjoy his conversation. He'd be one I'd have to be drunk to talk to."

"Blah, blah, blah. Just pick one already."

As Blithe orders her drink, a young, handsome G.I.L.F sits right next to me. He smells *amazing*! Like a sweet musk. I want to take him right there on the bar!

Settle down…

"OOO, look at that hot piece of man that just sat right next to you," Blithe whispers.

"I know! I see him Blithe. Try not to be so obvious."

As Blithe and I sip our drinks, we overhear him order a martini with maraschino cherries. *Lots* of maraschino cherries… Blithe and I shared a glance, both thinking the same thing.

"I think he may be into men." Blithe joked.

"That's too bad because he's a handsome piece of man candy!" I laugh.

"Hey ladies. . . Are you enjoying yourselves?"

As I turn toward the voice, I realize the question is coming from the man sitting next to me. Stunned by the question, I answered hesitantly.

"Umm… Yes. I come here a lot and have never been disappointed!"

"Good! I see you ladies are getting low on your cocktails. Should I refresh them?"

"No, I'm leaving to get home to my husband very soon, but you two enjoy yourselves!" Blithe says.

She finishes her martini almost instantly, pays her tab, and walks out the door.

"I'm Kaleb. What name can I put with your face?" He turns toward me.

"Very charming," I say. "The name is Franchesca!" tracing the rim of the glass with my fingertip.

Maybe he could be the one for the night.

"Nice to put a name with a familiar face. You look serious every time I see you, and I've never seen you laugh." he offers a crooked smile.

"Really? Well, if the occasion calls for laughter, then I will do so. So, you've seen me here a few times? Something must've made you remember me, unless you're taking lessons on how to be a stalker."

Who is this guy keeping tabs on my facial expressions? I hope he doesn't have a criminal background, or would that be more exciting?

"I notice all beautiful women. I'm a man... and the recurrence of a beautiful woman is hard to forget."

"Are you hitting on me, Kaleb?" lifting my eyebrows.

"Not at all, just telling it like I see it."

This was going well. I figured I would have him in my condo, or his in about an hour or two. The countdown starts *now*! I open my mouth to continue our potentially enticing conversation, but his cell phone ringtone interrupts before I get out the words. Luckily, he ignores it and I continue.

"Do you live in the area since you frequent my favorite lounge?"

"Your favorite, huh? Well, that's good to know. As a matter of fact, I do live close. I can't complain... The commute from home to work *is* pretty good!"

"How..." Another ring tone interruption. Maybe he has a girlfriend. He's too hot not to.

"I apologize, I'm here with a friend, and he's wondering where I am with his drink."

"Well, you better get back then," I say, hoping he will stay a bit longer or invite me over to his table.

"Yeah, I probably should. I wouldn't want to be rude. It was nice meeting you."

"So nice," I say with a smirk.

I watch him walk away in the gold-framed mirror behind the bar, and suddenly he turns around. I turn toward him.

"Before my phone rang, you were going to ask me something. What was it?"

"Oh, I was going to ask exactly how good your commute from home to work is?"

He laughs. "I own the place."

28

There goes the evening of events. I can't take the owner home once, then ditch him and think I'll still be welcomed back here. I like this place too much.

After finishing my second martini, I head to my condo, but can't get the thought of this charmer out of my head. Although, it was a short conversation, he left me wanting to know more about him. But that wasn't the reason I was there tonight. I want one thing and he left me with more than I bargained for.

***

The next morning, as I shift in bed, reaching for my phone to read the time, Blithe calls to inquire about my scheduled night for a loveless rendezvous.

"So, how was your night of passion?"

"There was no night of passion. He had a friend and stayed at the bar with him. I honestly didn't try, but I would like to forget him. Turns out he is the owner of Martini Life. He's been noticing me this entire time."

"If he's noticed you all this time, don't you think it's worth trying him again?"

"No. He's the owner of the bar. I can't 'one night' him, them go back to pick up other guys. Are you crazy?"

"But maybe he actually likes you."

"I don't need him to like me. I want him to lust for me!"

"You never want a guy to love you, or even like you for that matter. Franchesca, it's been four years since Xander broke you and you called off the engagement. It's time to let someone back in your heart."

"I'm over Xander. However, when a man leads you to believe he's in love with you, then you catch him *proposing* to his ex- girlfriend, you just want to be single for a while."

Blithe acts like she didn't experience the heartbreak with me. He didn't even have the courage to tell me that he moved on. I had to find *him*. We never spoke after the days of not eating, sheltering myself underneath my fuzzy blankets, and putting zero effort into my career. Hell, I lived with her and her husband for a year before I managed to salvage the remaining pieces of my will and dignity.

"Franchesca, right now, your life as an architect is you living at work and working from home. Your weekend recreational activities consist of luring guys back to your place. If I wasn't your best friend, I would think you were a sociopath."

"Don't analyze me with your psychology degree. But speaking of work, I have to get going, I have to pick up blueprints from your husband… remember him?"

"Just remember what I said 'Chesca."

"Yeah, I will. By the way, are you supposed to hate your best friend?"

"Only when you know she's right. Your high-rise, 20-story, work of art condo won't always keep you warm at night."

"That's debatable. What do you think goose-down comforters are for? See you tonight!" I hurry to hang up the phone.

Tonight is Blithe's birthday, she has been my best friend for seven years and I still don't know what to get her. So this year, I thought long and hard. I know she loves a city view and night life. So, I rented the rooftop of the Prudential Tower, where she can oversee the city through their 50-foot windows. I'm having her favorite dishes catered, then we'll travel to the Gypsy Bar, the poshest club in Boston. She *will* dress to impress!

After a busy day at the office, I realize it is already 6:00pm and I have no idea what to wear. Whatever I choose, it must be positively alluring. Something that hugs my body in all the right places, short enough to reveal my newly sculpted legs and a plunged neckline to capture the voluptuousness of my bust. I need them to want to see more! I have the perfect dress. It's light blue with sequins, backless and about five inches above the knee.

***

The Prudential Tower is nice! It almost looks like a ballroom, except there is no ceiling, only 50-foot windows surrounding the patio with white sparkling string lighting draping them. Several bouquets of fresh tulips and lilies that also have lights embedded around them. The flooring isn't the typical cement you see on the rooftop of a building. It's floral-painted and finished with an opaque, silver glittering epoxy. Making you feel like you're walking atop a magical garden!

The night is starting off to be great! I think this is a job well done. Blithe is having a good time and so am I, until she tries to play matchmaker at dinner. The Gypsy Bar is where my plan will unfold with a man of my choosing, not a setup that won't leave my side for the rest of the night. Blithe and her degree have made her believe she has the powers of a romantic profiler.

"Franchesca!" she yells from across the room. "I'd like you to meet Bill!"

30

Bill? He sounds boring. Probably another one of those guys who loves to talk about his life's' successes and pretends to be intrigued by the art in my profession. Somehow, they always manage to sway the conversation back to themselves and the intricacies of what makes food and wine, *fine*. I have *absolutely* no interest in self-centeredness, I want to scream to the world, but somehow, I manage to say…

"It's nice to meet you, Bill."

"Bill works with me at the office," Blithe adds.

"Yeah, I know. I was the one who invited your office, remember?"

"And now you finally get to meet! I'm going to mingle a bit. You two have fun. I'm sure you have lots to discuss."

I roll my eyes at her lack of subtlety. How dare she pull this crap right now? This guy isn't even my type and she knows it. I shoot her the worst look of disdain as she walks away, smiling. Leaving me in the center of the rooftop with a man waiting for me to show him attention. *Maybe I should change my facial expression to something a bit more pleasant.* I force a smile…

"Hi Bill. How did you enjoy the food?"

"It was eloquently selected. I especially liked the Wagyu steak, and the red wine seemed to partner well. Was it infused with truffles?"

Here we go. . . I stare him in the face as he continues to talk, trying not to display uninterest in my demeanor. Another pretentious man to bore me to death. Where the hell does Blithe find these guys?

When I snap back to reality, I check the time, and he has been yammering on for a minute and a half. Hopefully, he hasn't noticed I stopped listening. But something tells me if he had, he wouldn't care too much because the sound of his own voice seems to be self-soothing. I scan the room for someone to pawn him off on. I find her. She's perfect! Curly blonde hair, voluptuous breasts, and she writes for Food and Spirits Magazine. Based on this conversation, it would be a good match for me to make my escape.

"You know what, Bill?" I blurt. "I'm going to the restroom. Why don't you talk to Cynthia?" I gently grab her arm, drawing her closer, making direct eye contact with him. "Ask her if she's enjoying the food and wine choices you seem to like talking about so much."

I leave them to what they do best and look for Blithe to give her a piece of my mind. How dare she make decisions regarding my love life… or lack thereof.

"Blithe!" I aggressively whisper, making a B-line toward her. She turns to me with a wide smile and asks.

"Where's Bill?"

"Where's *Bill*? *That's* the first thing you notice? That he isn't attached to my hip. You want to know where he is? He's talking to Cynthia about topics that don't interest me at all."

"You pawned him off?"

"Absolutely! I don't want you to set me up with any more of your colleagues. It's like they're the same guy, just in a different disguise. One is tall and handsome, another is short and stocky, and the last one was a beefcake beauty, but they *all* bore me to sleep! You're not the Millionaire Matchmaker. You are a Psychologist. I know you think I'm in a labyrinth of loveless relationships but let me find my own guy."

"Fine, I'll mind my own business."

I sigh with relief. "Thank You."

***

It's 11pm, and we arrive at the Gypsy Bar, where the fun is about to begin! We see celebrities coming in and out. We had no idea it would be like this. The front of the building is about 200 feet high and has pillars like the White House, except this *house* is beige. Oscillating spotlights illuminate the club, as you enter. It looks so prestigious. I'm glad I reserved a booth ahead of time. Otherwise, we would be standing in the entry line for hours. This was going to be the most memorable birthday for Blithe.

After we check-in with security and the concierge, Blithe, her husband, and I sit in our booth and request bottle service from our personal waitstaff.

"Look at all the eye candy in this place, Franchesca! I'm sure you won't have any trouble finding a guy!"

"I *KNOW*! I don't know where to start. I'll just let my looks work for me and see what Santa brings me!"

Blithe's husband, Terry steals her to the dance floor, while I grab my drink and search the scene for potentials. I see two guys at the bar talking, smiling, and looking my way. I smile back and finish enjoying my martini, hoping they'll visit my table. When I look up, one of the gentlemen is already on his way to me. Tall, handsome, slender, and definitely my type.

"Excuse me, but I noticed you were alone and thought you would enjoy some company."

"I'm actually here with friends for a birthday party, but I don't mind if you join me."

"Sure." He smiles. "I'm Sebastian. My friend and I were just talking about how beautiful you look."

"Thank you! Sometimes I try a little harder than others!" As Sebastian sits down to join me, I hear my name being called. I look up to see I see Bill.

"Franchesca, there you are. I missed you before we left the restaurant."

Bill stands next to me only to introduce himself to the man whose company I was beginning to enjoy.

 "I'm Bill… and *you* are?"

"The names' Sebastian… Franchesca, I apologize. I didn't know you were here with someone."

"This is a colleague of my best friend. He's here for the party." I quickly reply. "Bill, why are you looking for me? Is there something wrong?"

"No, there's nothing wrong. I just want to finish our conversation."

"There will be plenty of time for that, but at the moment, I'm engaged in conversation with Sebastian."

"Oh sure. I will enjoy it as well!" taking a seat next to me.

The audacity of this man. Does he think Sebastian and I are looking for group conversation? How did Bill even get in here? The line outside was ridiculous without a reservation. I just wish he and his lovely toupee would go enjoy someone else's conversation. Where the heck is Cynthia when you need her? What exactly is he trying to do? Intercept me from being interested in anyone else? But what can I say? *Get the hell out of here, you, boring imbecile.* Of course, I can't. That would be rude.

"So, Sebastian, are you going to invite your friend over? He looks a little lonely at the bar by himself."

"Sure, I'll be right back."

I watch as he walks to the bar. Completely forgetting that Bill is sitting next to me. Sebastian exchanging words with his friend and the bartender piques my curiosity. Because they are also passing glances at me. Finally, they return to the table, but Sebastian has two drinks in his hand, and so does his friend.

"I'm Sebastian's friend Alex. I got you another martini as a thank you for inviting me to your table."

"Thank you. And Sebastian… is that second drink for Bill?" I ask.

He laughs. "No, it's for you because I like your smile."

"Thank you! You two are very sweet and are clearly trying to get me to loosen up a bit!"

"So... either of you gentlemen want to dance?"

I see Bill stand up out of my peripheral vision, but I continue to stare at Alex and Sebastian hoping one of them will be brave enough to accept my invitation. After a moment, Alex grabs my hand to pull me to the dance floor.

He's a gentleman as we dance. He doesn't try to grope me. He just wants to dance, which is so refreshing. He was good at it, too staying with the rhythm and most importantly, keeping up with me. Dancing with me is a test because I'm a sexy beast on the dance floor, and I never know my next move.

I don't realize 20 minutes have passed; I'm having so much fun! That's when Sebastian comes to take over as my dance partner. Sebastian is as much of a sexy dancer as I am. He sways his body side to side while lowering into a squatting position, outlining my curves with his hands, but never quite touching my body. He quickly spins me just to catch me in his masculine arms. I love it when he holds me close. Sebastian is firm, seductive, and I can smell his intoxicating cologne. I know who I want to take home, but that isn't the hard part. It's getting him away from Alex. If he isn't willing, I know I can just postpone our engagement.

"That was great! You're an amazing dancer!" I yell over the music.

"Thanks, but I think it was you making me look good!"

"Before we go back to the table, what are you doing tomorrow afternoon?"

I take a step closer to him and rest both palms on his chest.

"Nothing much, I'm available."

"I've been waiting to go to this new brunch spot opening in my neighborhood and you seem like a good person to take. How about keeping me company while I eat?"

"It's a date! I mean... It's not a date, but...What time and where?" he stammers.

"I could call you in the morning. What's your number?"

Soon after I enter his number in my cell, Blithe call to tell me that the evening is coming to an end and they're leaving.

"Sebastian, do you know of any after-parties tonight, or are you just heading home? I don't want you to be too hungover for brunch tomorrow?"

"No after-parties. I'm just going to relax. I think I've had enough to drink tonight."

***

I leave the bar unable to contain my excitement on the drive home because my plan is about to unfold. It's been about three weeks since I've been ravaged, and I'm *definitely* due! An hour passes, so I pick up my phone and dial Sebastian. He answers...

"This is Sebastian."

His voice offers alluring bravado.

"Hey, I heard there was an after-party in Cambridge. It's a sexy party! Laid back, dim lighting and they only serve wine at this hour. You interested?

"Franchesca?" he questions.

"Of course!"

"Sure, but I just dropped off Alex."

"That's no bother. I was hoping it would be the two of us.

"Where's the party?"

"237 Valentine Court, Cambridge. Just plug it into your GPS. It's the 20th floor, suite 2008. See you *real* soon."

After half an hour, I hear a knock at the door, and I'm ready to reveal my seductive prowess. I chose my lingerie carefully. I want his first impression of me to be irresistible. I oil my skin to a shimmery gleam and am dressed in a red and black corset. The one with lace around the breasts and the ties in the back to lift them to their perkiest. And covering my voluptuous bottom is a pair of red lace panties that allow my cheeks to fall just enough to make any man want to reach for them, accompanied by a black garter belt and thigh-high nylons. When I open the door for him, I don't want to be completely exposed, so I pull on my red satin robe that drapes over all my curves right down to the floor. When he sees me in it, he can view the outline of my perfectly sculpted bottom, as I walk away luring him into the bedroom.

I open the door...

"Hello, Sebastian," I coo.

He stands in the hallway with a look of enticed shock on his face, staring me down from head to toe and back again.

"*Wow!*" He drools. "I thought there was going to be an after party, but here you are opening the door looking... looking... I apologize. You've stopped my ability to form complete sentences."

"Would you like to come in?"

He walks in, never taking his eyes off me, and sits on my sofa, very still, very captivated by what's in his sights, too fascinated to look away.

Even though he knows he probably should.

"You're awfully quiet, Sebastian. Is it too late for playful banter?" I ask while pouring him a glass of Chardonnay.

"Not at all. This is just a pleasant surprise. Very unexpected."

I sit on the couch, giving him the glass, watching his eyes as they follow my breasts. I gently lift his chin to align his gaze with mine and say...

"Why don't you have some Chardonnay to get your mind off things."

He tips his glass to his lips only to finish it all at once. Once I see his actions, I follow suit. I place my hand on his chest and push him gently so he will relax on the sofa. As I brush my hands through his soft brown hair, I stand in front of him and drop my satin robe to the floor. His arms reach out for me and touch my thigh. I lean inward toward him, and begin to whisper in his ear...

"Is this too much for you?"

I kiss him, stealing his breath away. He runs his fingers through my shoulder-length locks, giving me goosebumps as he kisses the base of my neck.

Now *my* breath is shortened.

He grabs me firmly in handfuls, caressing me like I'm a small kitten. I'm relaxing like one too. I don't want him to stop. It is so euphoric that my eyes begin to close. The thought of keeping him for more than just tonight crosses my mind. I feel the sweat bead on my chest as the fire ignites in my body. My heart-beat races...

I watch him as he undresses. His body is chiseled and tan, he has such a beautiful structure. I want to touch him, but I am in a daze.

Our night of passion ends just as quickly as it began, but not in a disappointing sense.

"Thank you for a *wonderful* end to the evening, Sebastian!"

"Oh...is that your subtle way of asking me to leave?"

"A little." I chuckle. "I have to be up in six hours."

"Are we still on for brunch?"

"Oh. Brunch." Hoping he had forgotten my initial ploy to lure him to my condo. "I know I'm not going to get much sleep tonight. I need to shower and prepare for meetings. I'll probably be too tired for brunch. Raincheck?"

"Sure. No problem."

He dresses in an upbeat manner and walks toward the door. I open it and we say goodnight for that last time. When I close the door behind him, I look through the peephole, only to find him pacing nervously. He seems to be trying to gain enough courage to knock on my door once more, but he doesn't.

Chapter 3

The Tangled Web

39

Opting not to go back to Martini Life after my last week, I chose a different spot in the Party district. At the Rouse, the music is a bit louder than I'm used to, and it's not as cozy. Seems more like grunge, but what the hell? I'll check it out. After I grab a seat, my first sight is a tall, slender, fair-skinned man wearing glasses, a black motorcycle jacket, some kind of video game tee, and denim. Not the type I normally go for, but who am I kidding? I don't have a type and not really looking for anyone who would be classified as such. A hot guy I can have for the evening *is* my type!

For now, anyway.

It's completely superficial, but that's the lane I've been forced into. This guy looks like a taller version of Mark Wahlberg, and I can get into that. But I can tell by how he interacts with his friends; he's just a bit cocky. He demands attention and taking over the conversation. Watching him vividly from across the room, I almost see this as a challenge. An opportunity to show my dominance and take what I want.

As I place one Manolo on the floor to bring myself to both feet, drink in hand and ready to make a play. A woman glides over to my tall, handsome man and places her hand on his lower back. He has no reaction as she approaches, almost as if she isn't there.

They can't be an item…

Time to make my move. I walk sexily toward him and pretend to trip, only to spill my Cosmopolitan all over her white dress.

"UGH!" she gasps. "Look at what you've done!"

"I apologize. It was truly an accident. Let me bring you some club soda."

"There's not enough club soda in this bar to get this out!"

"Here's my business card. Send me the bill for the dry cleaning. No harm, no foul."

"I'm leaving. I'll see you guys later."

She snatches the card from my hand and storms out. I turn toward the handsome man, and as I open my mouth to speak, he laughs hysterically. I stop in my tracks with a stunned look on my face, wondering if I'm the butt of the joke.

"Umm, did I miss something?"

"Sorry. That was my ex-girlfriend, and I've been trying to get her to leave all night, and it seems you've just answered my prayers! And for *that*, I thank you! Frankly, she deserves it! She only bought that dress to try to entice me and was planning to return it after tonight. *Now* she's stuck with it. Karma's a – well, ya know!"

"*Oookay*, doesn't seem like that relationship ended very well."

"It didn't. It's a saga to tell. I wouldn't want to bore you with a bedtime story."

"You're probably right, but my bedtime isn't for hours. So, enlighten me."

I'll give him any reason to keep engaging with me.

"Long story short, we dated off and on for two years. Every time we were off, she came back in just enough time to make my life, and the life of the woman I was seeing, a living hell. This girl has a couple of screws loose. I can't be with a girl like that."

"That sounds like a big history. Good thing you're still friends." I chuckle.

"So, what's *your* story?"

What's *my* story? What would make him think I have any type of *story?* Have I been walking around with a name tag that reads, "Hello, my name is Heartbroken?" I wear expensive attire to disguise that fact. I don't want anyone to know me or think they know me. There's only one person in this world who has that luxury. Blithe. If this is his way of trying to get to know me, my brick wall has been built, and it's not coming down. So, my response is. . .

"I don't have one."

"C'mon, a pretty woman like you has to have a story."

"Mine ended four years ago, and *now* anything casually romantic is just a blur."

"Bullshit, but I'll take it."

"Like you have a choice." I chuckle.

"So where are all your friends tonight?" he asks.

"I'm alone. Sometimes it's nice to go out, enjoy the music, and people watch."

"*Ooooh*! I see! *That's* your story. You're an alcoholic!?"

I step into his personal space as his friends surround him, out of earshot.

"*Haha*, you're a funny guy Mr. . . I pause for him to finish my sentence.

"Jamaal."

"Okay Jamaal, A.K.A. smartass! I'm Franchesca. Do you want to accompany me to the bar? Manolo's aren't exactly made for their comfort."

"Manolo's, eh? I could take one of your shoes right now, get $500 and buy you 7 pair of comfortable shoes!"

We both laugh. When the laughter stops, he turns it into a coy little smile as he gazes into my eyes. For just a moment, I catch myself doing the same.

What am I doing?

"Are you ok?" I interrupt the gaze.

"Yeah… It's that you have pretty eyes… and a pretty face… um… and a beautiful smile." clears his throat.

"Well, you're not bad looking either."

"Would you like to go on a date with me, Franchesca?"

A DATE?! What does he think this is? Love Connection? It's more like Elimi-date. I eliminate all possibilities of dating you. What do I say? He's sweet and nice, but I'm not looking for any commitments. After all that mind-numbing banter between me and my thoughts, I finally come up with a response.

"Sure, I'll go out with you."

"How about tomorrow?" he asks.

I lean over to whisper. . .

"How about tonight? It's still early. Let's go back to my place for a little nightcap. Here's my address; I'll see you in an hour."

After jotting down my address on the back of my card, I gently place it in his hand, and walk toward the door. I look over my shoulder to give him a wink and a smile. He smiles right back!

***

An hour should be enough time for Jamaal to say good night to his friends and for me to have a shower. But somehow my timing is off because the doorbell rings as soon as the water hits my body. Removing myself from the shower, I casually walk to the door. Looking through the peephole, I recognize Jamaal.

I open the door dripping from head to toe, and part my glossed lips to form the words,

"Hey, I wasn't expecting you so soon."

Looking from my eyes to my soaking feet, he asks.

"Is this a bad time?"

"No, but there's a draft. You could come inside or stay in the hall while I dry off."

He enters, never taking his eyes off me. *I seem to have that effect on people.*

"How about that nightcap?" I ask.

Walking to the kitchen, he starts to stammer. I'm unable to dissect what he's trying to say, so I quickly return with his cocktail. He finally mutters.

"I can't believe this is happening."

"Believe it, Jamaal… and forget everything else. You belong to me right now."

He smirks and sits comfortably on the sofa, licking his lips. I know the urge is there to place them on mine, but he resists.

"I don't mind if you have a nibble," I suggest.

He consumes his drink non-stop until it is empty and places the glass calmly on the table behind me. He then looks into my eyes, and in one motion, grabs the back of my neck with one hand and kisses my lips. So soft. So tender. Pleasure and passion overcome me.

"You taste so sweet!" he pants. "Like an orchard of ripened strawberries."

Kissing my neck and traveling to my shoulder, he whispers.

"It seems I interrupted your shower. Why don't I help you with that."

I guide him to the still-running shower and undress him. His body is lean, as if he works out four times a week and eats salmon and salad just for fun. I take a moment to admire his sculpture. Running my hands from his plump chest to his muscle-toned abs. My mind wonders to thoughts of everything we could do for each other.

The moment we step into the streaming water, there are no words, just the sound of the pitter-patter of water hitting our bodies. It's warm, and I somehow feel protected in his arms. He turns me away from him and starts soaping my backside with my pumice loofa.

"I wanted to make sure you finished your shower." Giving me a wink.

I can't speak. After he soaps and rinses my body, he dries me, then carries me to the bedroom.

"I know your feet are tired from your workout in those Manolo's. Let me rub them for you."

My body is too weak to resist, so, I allow him to touch my feet. However, my mind is racing. I always insist they leave and not treat me like a love interest. Has this *actually* become that thing called a "date?" *What is he thinking? And why haven't I taken control of this situation?* As the sensation in my feet begins to heighten, my thoughts fade into nothingness, and I realize I'm drifting off to sleep.

***

The piercing sound of my alarm clock disrupts my slumber. Remembering last night, I quickly check next to me to see if Jamaal took the liberty of staying over.

He didn't.

What a relief.

But there's a note…

> *Franchesca, you looked so peaceful sleeping. I didn't want to wake you.*
>
> *I had an amazing night with you, and I hope to see you again very soon!*
>
> *How about dinner at my place? Call Me*
>
> *Jamaal*

Blithe always has a knack for video calling me before I go to work. As if I'm not doing anything important during that time. I answer the ringing phone…

"Yes Blithe, what can I do for you this morning?"

"Hey there, lovely! I know last night was 'date night' and I was wondering if you caught something in your web?"

"I caught Jamaal, actually. He was sweet and tender and left a note saying he wanted to see me again. What the hell is that about?"

"So, are you going to see him?"

"Of course!... *NOT*! What kind of guy sleeps with a woman, bathes her, then wants to date her? He's friggin' backwards, it was a one-night stand. He should be moving on to the next girl and bragging to his buddies about how awesome it was."

"Wait! Wait! Are you telling me he bathed you? That's so sweet! I haven't been bathed by my husband in who knows how long. Why won't you go out with him?"

"Come on, Blithe, you know me. Dating is just not in the cards right now. It's too much drama and hurt. I like things just the way they are. I get the guy, fulfill my womanly needs and get rid of him. It's simple, no strings, no hassle!"

"Don't you wonder what it would feel like to fall in love again, but this time, with the right guy? You can't be fulfilled."

"No… Sometimes… I don't know. I try not to let those thoughts consume me. I like the loveless copulation part. It's much more fun to think about!"

Blithe rolls her eyes. "Okay, bye. There's no reasoning with your psychosis, but I won't give up."

I smile and hang up the receiver. I know she is just looking out for me and wants me to have what I thought I had in my last relationship. She's been so lucky. Blithe found the love of her life on the first try, and he's wonderful! But, as for me, I don't even know what dating would even be like or how to do it correctly anymore.

As I walk into my office building, I hear lots of commotion, arguing, screaming and profanity. Walking towards the elevator, I take a closer look, and the woman being restrained looks very familiar. Security spots me and yells. . .

"Ms. Veranda! This woman says she's here to see you about dry cleaning. I told her you hadn't arrived yet and she started screaming obscenities."

I follow security to the woman and realize she's the one whose dress I ruined the night before.

"Yes officer, I *actually am* taking care of her dry cleaning. But… miss, if you continue to make a spectacle, I'll have security escort you out, never to be welcomed back again. Now, can they release you, or do you need continued restraint?"

"I'm fine, thank you. And my name is Katia. Here is the dress you're paying for" she declares.

"Thank you for delivering it, but you could've left it at the front desk with a return address."

"*Oh. . . NO!* I had to see your face, so I could see what you look like after telling you, you were with my boyfriend!"

"Excuse me?"

"Last night, I followed Jamaal, thinking I would surprise him when he arrived home only to see he ended up at your place. He didn't leave for hours! I realized it was you when I saw you exit the car. What does that even mean? Did you enjoy being with another woman's boyfriend?" Katia scolds.

"According to Jamaal, he has no girlfriend, so you can take that up with him, *and* we're done here. Should I have security escort you out?"

I leave her standing in the middle of the room and head to my office, fuming over the situation. I will call my dry cleaner for a pick-up to have this dress completed by the time my day is over. I think I just might have that dinner with Jamaal after all.

***

The date is set. After work, I pick-up the dry cleaning and head over to Jamaal's when I realize I'm being followed… Again. I become angry all over again! I arrive at his home, barely able to keep my composure. I reach into my backseat to retrieve the dress and knocked on the door.

"Hi! I'm so glad you're here. I have five courses for us to share together. I hope you like it!" He exclaimed.

"It smells fantastic, which is better than I can say my morning was."

"How so? Tell me about your day."

"Well, I walk into work, and a crazed woman was being restrained by security, wanting to see me."

"Did you know her?"

"Not that well. I gave her my card once. The crazy thing is, I found out she followed a friend to my house once, and now she knows where I live."

"Wow, she sounds like a lunatic. Did you ever find out what she wanted?"

"Oh yeah! She just wanted to know how I thought her boyfriend was in bed."

"What?!"

"Yeah. . . The woman I speak of, her dry cleaning is in the bag. Why don't you open it and take a look."

Confused, he walks toward the bag to open it. Once he sees the dress inside, he quickly turns to me.

"I think her name is Katia. Is that correct, Jamaal? Am I pronouncing that right?" I demand.

His eyes widen.

"I don't know what to say, Franchesca."

"I do!... Clean this mess up and enjoy your dinner."

I storm out the front door, start the ignition, then screech my tires out of his driveway. On my way home, I ignore two calls from Jamaal, then he finally texts.

Franchesca, I'm sorry. I was so dumb founded by your story
I couldn't say anything. She is crazy, and I can't seem to stop her.
She interferes with everything when I try to move on. I don't know what to do.

My reply:

"I would get a lawyer. I'm an architect. I can't help you."

Chapter 4

Unlikely Story

49

I consider buying a taser in the event Miss Katia decides she wants to provoke me further. On the other hand, I figure she can't be that much of a threat if she hasn't been arrested. This is part of the reason I don't do relationships. The unnecessary drama. It's like volunteering for intermittent suffocation. Who wants that?

After a good night's sleep, knowing I avoided future mayhem, I enjoy my morning coffee. Flavored with hazelnut, I inhale the lovely aroma as I stare out the window at the busy street below, wondering where all the people are going. Considering what adventures they may be on.

My phone rings. An unknown number flashes on the screen. I stare at the number, debating answering it, but I never pick up calls I don't recognize. They never seem to be worth my time. Half the time, it's sales calls or some scam artist. I decide to ignore it and return to my morning bliss of people-watching. My imagination begins to peak, until I'm interrupted by a knock at the door. *No one wants me to enjoy my morning.* I roll my eyes and approach the door to look through the peephole, ready to pretend I'm not home if it's anyone I don't care to see.

It's Kaleb.

The owner of Martini Life.

I haven't been there in a month. What could he want? I don't open the door from skepticism; Instead, I speak through it.

"Kaleb, what are you doing here? Are you positive you aren't stalking me?"

He laughs. "I'm pretty sure I'm not. I want to come by to give you your driver's license. You left it the last time you were at the bar. I'm surprised you didn't come back to get it."

Oh! Feeling relief, I open the door.

"Thanks for bringing it by, but you didn't have to go through all that trouble. I have a couple old ones."

"Well, now you have another!" he jokes.

We share a laugh followed by an awkward gaze.

"Well, I just wanted to drop that off to you. I have to run a few errands for a tailgate at the Red Sox game."

"That sounds fun! Believe it or not, I've never been to a baseball game."

"I'm meeting a couple friends, but one backed out, so we have an extra ticket. I'd love to be the first one to show you a good time and how to properly celebrate the Red Sox!

Do I want to give up my afternoon of relaxation for the Red Sox? Most people would jump at the chance, but I'm standing here pondering like a teenage introvert with a lack of social skills. But the last thing I want, is for him to think this is more than what it is.

Nothing.

But, I could *actually* have fun. That would be personal growth Blithe could revel in.

"Just to be clear, this is *not* a date. And promise me you aren't one of those crazed fans you hear about on the news who starts fights over foul balls."

"I promise. Unless the other guy can't respect that I had the ball first!"

"Oh lord!" Rolling my eyes. "Come in so I can get ready."

I walk to my bedroom thinking… *What do I own that would be appropriate for a ball game?* I own stilettos, suits, workout wear, and cocktail dresses. Who knew there was such an event where my wardrobe wouldn't be acceptable? Finally deciding, after flinging half my closet across the room. I decide to wear black leggings, a slightly shimmery, an opaque grey tee with a red tank underneath and my leopard print peep toe sling backs! Perfect and comfortable! I emerge from the bedroom and I hear hysterical laughter.

I stop in my tracks.

"What in the world is so *damn* funny!"

"Your outfit… It's hilarious! Don't get me wrong, you look great. But I can definitely tell you've never been to a baseball game!"

We both laugh.

"Well, this is the closest thing I had for the event. I don't own a pair of tennis shoes, and it's too hot for jeans. So, do you want to continue to laugh at my expense, or should we get on the road?"

***

We arrive at the ball-park a couple of hours early to do this thing called "tailgating." Of course, I'd heard of it back in college, but I never participated. I was more of a book worm. So today is the day I learn what it's all about. We park and walk what seems like a mile in my heels until we run into Kaleb's friend.

"This is my buddy, Jeff."

"Wow, you never told me you had a beautiful woman in your life!"

"Nice to meet you, Jeff. I'm Franchesca."

Jeff offers me a seat and an ice cold beer. Just the right thing for this hot day. Although, a margarita would be the best thing! I sip my beer and gaze at all the traffic and the brute activity taking place around me. Everyone is having a great time! All are dressed in team memorabilia, bumping chests, drinking, and eating hot dogs. It makes me chuckle, and I have the sudden urge to partake in the activities at hand. So, I stand tall from my seat…

"Let me take over the grill and you and Jeff entertain me with a chug battle!"

"What?" Kaleb asks, confused.

"It's your first beer *and* you own a bar. I'm sure you've built a tolerance for alcohol by now. Do it and I'll give you both a dollar. The winner gets two!" I laugh.

They both look at each other, grab a new beer and start to gulp at my countdown.

"CHUG! CHUG! CHUG!" I chant while jumping up and down.

After about five seconds, Kaleb dropped his empty can into the cooler, while Jeff took his last few swallows.

"Victory! Kaleb wins! I shout.

"Yup, now where's my two bucks!" he demands.

I reach into my bag for the money and jam it in his pocket.

"Now it's your turn," Kaleb replies.

"*Me?* Oh, I have to watch the meat. It's very sensitive, and it just might burn without my guidance."

"No excuses, missy," Jeff adds.

I stare at the can in Kaleb's hand, thinking, *I don't chug beer. I don't even drink it!* I've just been taking courtesy sips this entire time. What if I choke and spit all over Kaleb's face?! Then I gain enough courage to decide. Why not live in the moment? I've already done one thing I've never attempted today.

I stand there reluctantly as they yell dual chants of "DO IT! DO IT! DO IT!"

I snatch the beer from Jeff's hand, press my lips to the opening, and drink as fast as I can. They stare in amazement.

I'm actually doing it. I'm actually almost done! I pull the can from my lips, slam it on top of the grill, and unexpectedly release a huge belch.

"Wow, it's like you're one of the guys!" Kaleb jokes.

"That was a definite head rush. I liked it!"

I'm having a good time doing something I thought I would never do. Especially with a man I tried to victimize with my feminine prowess, and yet, I wasn't thinking about sex. It is a new feeling to not be consumed by my demons for once. Suddenly, my thoughts are disturbed by yelling in the distance. It's Jeff…

"Someone just fell backward off the top row of the stadium."

What? We run toward Jeff, and the whole tailgate crowd follows. There's pandemonium around the body lying on the pavement. I push through the crowd thinking my CPR training could come in handy. Both arms bent awkwardly in directions they shouldn't, and he has a bleeding wound on his head. He begins to groan.

Thank God he's alive!

Ambulances and police cars begin to pull up. Police disperse the crowd to give the wounded some room and privacy. The three of us walk away in awe, hoping the man will make a full recovery and his family will be there with him for comfort. The murmuring crowd travel back to their respective tailgate areas, including us. I grab a hotdog from the grill and plop down in the nylon folding chair, hoping the man gets the proper care. Several moments pass when we hear an announcement postponing the game due to the severe injury of the star player.

What was he doing up there?

Collectively, the crowd gasps at the announcement and people begin to make their way to the box office.

"That's insane and disappointing. I really wanted to show you your first Red Sox game."

"It's okay. For what it's worth, I had a great time tailgating. There will be more games and maybe you'll think of me."

Kaleb smiles. We wave goodbye to Jeff and retreat to the car for our journey back to the suburbs.

"It's still early, we could go back to my place to finish grilling the steaks, and I can make you your favorite cocktail!" he suggests.

"Sounds like a plan. Let's do it."

I sit in my seat like a deer in headlights, stunned by my choice of words. 'Let's do it…' *Why would I say that?* I hope he doesn't get the wrong idea. Well, then again, it wouldn't be a bad thing to roll around with him. . . *What am I thinking?* It would be terrible. Maybe I'd start to like him, and feelings would become mutual. Then we'd get physical, and feelings become stronger; the next thing you know, we're a couple. *NO WAY* am I getting tangled in *that* web.

As we pull into the driveway of his three-story modern bar loft, I break away from my thoughts. Walking in, there are hardwood floors clean enough to eat off. The scent of linen fills the air, and a chandelier in the living room casts glistening light on the rust-painted walls.

"I love your place. It feels so comfortable and unique! Want to trade?"

"Not a chance. I have it just the way I want it now. It took a while, but it's my masterpiece."

"This isn't exactly how I envisioned your place. It's more cultured than I would've guessed."

"Uh, thanks. . . I guess. What did you think it would be? Some dilapidated warehouse?

"Well, you did say it was on top of your bar. So, I just assumed it would be some small, dark, gloomy apartment with no décor or style."

"Oh, is that *all*. Didn't your mother teach you not to judge a book by its cover?"

"Um, no, I seemed to have missed that lesson or just completely ignored it. Besides, from the outside, you just see a bar. There could be anything up here, a storage unit or a place where vagrants hang out. Who knows!"

"*Now* you know what the two additional stories are. If you're done insulting me, would you like a drink or not?"

"Hit me with all you got!" I laugh.

Kaleb makes my drink and I sit on the patio as he grills the food from two feet away. The sun resting on my face is perfect, along with the aroma of a well-seasoned steak. My relaxing afternoon was actually happening. Who knew it would be with Kaleb?

"Franchesca, do you remember the night we met?"

"Yeah, I was attracted to you, but I thought you were gay." I chuckle.

"You thought I was gay? What the HELL gave you that impression?"

"What straight guy orders a drink and fills it up with maraschino cherries?"

"I hadn't eaten. It was more like a drink *and* a snack."

I tilt my head to meet my left shoulder as I offer him a smile of understanding.

"In retrospect, that's hilarious!" However, I apologize for my assumption. But what about that night?"

"Just the parts I haven't told you. I've watched you visit the bar every week wearing your finest; sitting at the bar as if you were waiting for something. Never seeing you smile often made me wonder if I could be the one to make that happen for you. I saw your face 17 times in my bar, and I never brewed enough courage to say anything, until that night. I didn't say much, but I knew I needed to say something, and when I saw you leave, it felt like I didn't say enough."

A lump begins to form in my throat at the sincerity in Kaleb's voice. My chest tightens at the thought of the next sentence that may exit his mouth.

"I *knew* you were a stalker, and apparently, I just made it incredibly easy for you."

"Seriously, I would like to take you out on an official date."

My eyes widen in disbelief. I've never had to reject someone in this way. Usually, I keep an unapproachable posture just to avoid people asking me out. I'm flattered, but I want to let him down easy, considering the saga he just ripped from his throat. I wasn't sure exactly where this conversation would lead, but it started in the "friend" zone and now it seems to be straddling the "dating" zone. *I did not sign on for this.* Why do men have to make everything complicated? I want to steer clear of relationships, but the little fat baby with the heart-shaped arrow keeps following me around. What do I do? I don't want to tell him the truth; it's clear he wants more than just the superficial. If I say yes to the date, Kaleb will assume I want him for his mind, and that's simply not true.

"Kaleb, I had a great time with you. You exposed me to some things I wouldn't have experienced, but I'm not ready for anything exclusive right now."

"I'm not asking for exclusivity, just a date."

I love how he says "just a date" as if it's some casual, fleeting activity that doesn't result in future sacrifice.

"Yeah, and dates turn into exclusivity." I oppose.

"Not if it turns out I don't like you. Look, you're making this more difficult than it has to be. Let's just decide to have fun together. How does that sound?"

"I can't argue with that."

I forcefully lower my eyelids, trying to prevent a noticeable eye roll at the fact that I just agreed to a situation that may end in disaster. I don't usually allow myself to be persuaded into potential regret.

What am I doing?

I should've been emphatic about my 'no.' I should've left immediately with a believable excuse. I manifest those all the time to get others to leave. Why couldn't I do it to provide an escape for myself? All I thought was to be nice to the man who has shown me kindness. Maybe it won't backfire.

56

Chapter 4
The Chase

It's been a week since I last saw Kaleb; thinking of that day together has made me smile a lot, but that doesn't negate my vow to non-exclusivity. Pondering over my decision, I somehow feel I've been bamboozled. He says, "Lets' just have fun," but he wants to date. How does that make sense? I'm not interested in dating. However, I agreed to the "fun." This situation makes me uneasy, but I haven't heard from him, so maybe he cooled off. I have a few minutes before my office day begins, so I call Blithe to gab about my adventure…

"Franchesca, my dear, to what do I owe the pleasure?"

"What's with the homemaker phone greeting? You sound like my grandmother. Are your in-laws in town pressuring the facade of a perfect wife?"

"You always know, don't you."

This is the other thing about relationships. If you're lucky enough to be together long enough and survive the obstacles of partnership, you inherit another set of parents. I have enough trouble battling my own on a weekly basis with their overbearing nature. Some people would consider this a blessing, but I am not *some* people.

"I called because I figured I'd give you some news, but don't get too excited."

"Spill it. I've got about 20 minutes before the in-laws come looking for me."

"Do you remember about three weeks ago I told you about the owner of Martini Life? Well, he unexpectedly showed up at my place, ended up hanging out for the day and made me dinner and cocktails."

"Oh my! Did you have an amazing roll in the hay? Was he good?"

"Whoa, Blithe. Calm down," I interrupt.

"Sorry… I haven't been intimate since the in-laws have been in town. Your stories are the closest thing to getting any excitement for a bit."

We both laugh…

"Actually, we didn't fool around. Surprisingly, I didn't have the urge. It was the best day I had with a guy in a long time. *But then,* he asked me on a date."

"Well, what did you say? You said yes, right?" Blithe exclaims,

"You would love that, wouldn't you? I told him I wasn't ready for a relationship and he proposed we just have fun. I wouldn't be able to treat this one like all the others."

"Why not? They're all just a piece of meat for you to devour for personal gain."

"Blithe! I can't sleep with him because I know he would start to develop feelings, and I just can't have that."

"What would be the most horrible thing about allowing a handsome, established, chivalrous, charming man to fall for you?"

"The worse thing? I'd get hurt because he wasn't who he seemed to be."

"Love is the ultimate game in life. Franchesca, it's like going to the casino. You enter it hopeful, and take a gamble; sometimes it pans out, and sometimes it doesn't. That's when you take the loss, learn from your mistake and try again with the knowledge gained. Did you ever think that by the time you're done pushing every man away, there won't be any left when you're ready for a relationship? Whether you attempt love now or later, the same risks still apply, and those guys that want to love you *now,* may be loving someone else, leaving you with nothing."

"You're very profound, Dr. Phil." I joke.

"I'm serious 'Chesca. You've been playing this game for two years. I understand you don't want to get hurt, and keeping your emotions at bay is much easier than facing them, but when will it end?"

"*I DON'T KNOW!* When I'm ready, or when the right guy inadvertently brings my wall down."

"*OH SHOOT!* 'Chesca, I have to go. The in -laws are coming. I don't want to be caught slipping because, apparently, you don't have personal friends when you're married, only collaborative ones! Love ya!"

The abrupt click in my ear is a clear indicator the call has ended. To some degree, I know Blithe is right, but I can't get my heart to agree.

Moments later, my phone rings. It's Jamaal, and thoughts run through my mind about whether to answer.

"Hi." I greet dryly.

"Hey Franchesca. It's Jamaal."

"Yeah, I know. What can I do for you?"

"I want to start again, start fresh with everything."

"It depends on if you've dealt with that problem of yours."

"We spoke and we have a mutual understanding."

"I think the two of you need counseling because she lives in a fantasy, and you seem to be oblivious."

"Let me take you to Marliave, it's an Italian restaurant. Consider it my apology and appreciation for a second chance! Should I pick you up at 6:30?"

"I don't do second chances, but I do like apologies. Fine, I'll see you later."

Work has been hectic lately. Trying to finish out the third quarter with exceptionally high numbers is exhausting. I need a drink more than usual after a rough day, and luckily it is almost five o'clock when my day comes to a close. As I drive home, Italian starts to sound more and more exciting than it did when the idea was first presented. Before any food or drink hits my lips, a shower is a necessity.

Entering my place, I throw my bags down, leaving a trail of clothes leading to the bathroom. I lay on the bed of the tub while the shower blades of water trickled down my stomach. Thoughts of the seduction I had in this tub, in this shower, make my muscles tighten. I want Jamaal this very moment, but he isn't due for another hour. I can't wait, so I enjoy my own company. Feeling 100% satisfied, I stay motionless for just a moment before lathering my body to prepare for an early dinner. Italian and Jamaal.

***

Sitting down for dinner, I realize my body is still raging from thoughts of the passion present at our first encounter. I stare at him with desire in my eyes.

"Franchesca, are you ok?"

I giggle, "I'm great! I just have a lot on my mind."

"Do you want to tell me about it?"

"Not particularly, but I'll definitely show you later."

"Okay. I want to apologize for the disruption my past has brought you. I want you and I to have a fresh start so you can get to know me and not my past."

"All is forgiven, as long as it doesn't happen again, and you can keep your chihuahua on a leash."

The waiter approached our table to recite the specials for the evening. They all sound delicious, so Jamaal orders every one of them. He wants me to have everything I want, but what I want is definitely *not* on the menu at Marliave.

When we're alone once again, I stand from the table and whisper in his ear.

"Meet me in the men's room in two minutes, no questions. . . two minutes."

I walk to the men's room, hoping it will be vacant with no wandering eyes from the dining room. Reaching the corridor, I place one hand on the men's restroom door, attempting to enter with a slight push. Suddenly, I hear the voice of a woman coming out of the ladies' room.

"Excuse me, miss, the ladies' room is over this way."

I keep my back turned toward the voice, hoping she'll walk away, but she continues to stand there, glaring at me as if she knew what I was planning. Slowly turning towards her, I forced a smile and a look of ignorance.

"Wow, that would've been embarrassing. Thank you for noticing I was going into the wrong restroom. Apparently, reading isn't my strong suit."

She chuckles and quickly exits the corridor to return to the dining room. I, on the other hand, continued my business. Entering the men's room, I hide in the last stall, patiently waiting for my excursion to begin. Shortly after, Jamaal enters the stall, and I start kissing his lips as if it were a race.

Then the men's room entrance door swings open, hitting the marble wall behind it.

BOOM! Making the sound of a small bomb going off.

I gasp in horror. *Did someone notice me walking in? Is someone just having a bad date?* I didn't know what to think. Jamaal and I remain in the last stall. We have no idea what to do, but staying silent seems like the best option.

Then an angry woman yells.

"*I KNOW YOU'RE IN HERE! COME OUT AND FACE ME LIKE A MAN!*"

Jamaal and I look at each other in disbelief. *Is that command for Jamaal?* He continues to stare at me and whispers. "I think that's Katia."

I silently mouth, "What is she doing here?"

Jamaal hunches his shoulders, accompanying the gesture with a look of confusion.

We wait.

The sound of the first stall being opened with brute force startles me again. Then the sound of the second and third doors slamming comes immediately after. Knowing there is only one more door to open before she reaches us in the last stall, Jamaal tilts his head back, seeming to collect his thoughts, and smooths his tailored suit with his hands. He unlatches the door, opens it with his right hand and steps out of the stall leading with his left leg. He closes his eyes and tilts his head back once more before looking at the woman, then opens his mouth to speak in an aggravated tone.

"Katia, what the in the——." He and the woman stare at each other in a moment of surprise. "Do I know you?"

She clears her throat. "Apparently not. I was looking for——, it doesn't matter. I apologize for barging in like a crazy person."

I peek through the slender crack in the stall door, and see him lower his eyebrows as he scrunches his face in bewilderment. "Yeah… no problem."

The woman leaves the men's room in a hurry, leaving a trail of expensive high-heel clicks behind.

I jump out of the last stall with my heart still racing. "*That's* the woman that gawked at me until I physically walked into the ladies room."

Jamaal widens his eyes. "Maybe she was looking for *you*." Holding his hand to his mouth, trying not to laugh.

I stand beside him, putting my left hand on his shoulder before bursting into laughter. This is the most ridiculous scenario I've ever been in. Including the year I got my arm stuck down the toilet trying to retrieve Blithe's bracelet back in college.

We gather ourselves and return to the dining room as our food arrives. *Perfect timing.* We sit in our seats. Jamaal facing the entrance. Something about always needing to see what's going on and who's coming in.

Right after placing his napkin on his lap, his expression turns from happy to confused.

"What's wrong Jamaal?"

"Nothing," he says nervously.

He quickly gets to his feet, almost taking the tablecloth with him. His smile is forced, then turns into an emotionless expression, then back to an insincere grin.

"Are you feeling ok?" continuing to enjoy my meal.

"Yeah… I— I'll be right back." He immediately walks away.

Jamaal's abrupt nervousness piques my curiosity, so I follow him with my eyes as he leaves the table. He stops to speak to a woman, but I can't see her face or hear the words being spoken. I think nothing of it and return to my stuffed mushrooms.

"Sorry about that. I had to take care of something." Jamaal reports as he returns to his seat.

"Is it a problem with the food?"

"No. I just needed to talk to someone I thought I knew. I think I need one more trip to the men's room," he says, leaving me with a wink.

I smile back almost lovingly. Then quickly snap out of it, shaking my head. *What am I doing?*

Shortly after Jamaal's absence, I reach for an Italian meatball on his plate and I look up to see Katia standing at our table.

"What the hell are you doing here?!" Whispering angrily.

"I'm here to see Jamaal," she says with a smug grin.

"You don't need to see Jamaal. He doesn't want to see you. But if you're hungry, we could leave you a doggie bag in the parking lot. You can identify with leftovers, can't you?" My snide retort matches her face.

"You think you're *so* smart?"

"Well…Yes… I'd like to say the same about you, but your actions have proven otherwise. I would label you as psychotic. What do you really want?" I ask.

"Just to let you know, not to get comfortable. Jamaal and I are always on and off. Soon enough he will come to his senses, and we will be together again. So, don't get too cozy in my chair."

"Oh, sweetie! Your chair has been replaced and upgraded. Why don't you leave before you embarrass yourself? Unless you would like me to do it for you."

Chuckling as she walks toward the entrance.

How dare she invite herself to an event she shouldn't have been privy to? Do I have a case of major lunacy on my hands? What type of stalker is she? More importantly, why am I pondering any of these things at all? Jamaal said he had this situation under control, but its clear he has blinders on. This is not my problem to deal with. I'm DONE! Like I said before, I'm an architect and its evident he needs the authorities for this mess and a shrink while he's looking.

Jamaal returns to the table, refreshed and polished.

"Everything looks great. Let's eat!"

"Let's not. Actually, you eat. I'm leaving."

"Wait! What's going on, Franchesca? I'm confused."

"Let me clear things up then. Katia took the liberty of gracing me with her unwanted presence and told me how you two are soul mates. Don't get me wrong, I can handle myself, but what I shouldn't be handling, is your fatal attraction. Furthermore, you knew she was here, and lied to my face. I've had enough of her and enough of you. Do yourself a favor… be a man and grow a pair!"

I can't continue the evening exchanging playful banter under false pretense. The waiter returns to check on us and I have him box my meal.

"Franchesca, please! Let's salvage the rest of the night."

"I can't. I asked you to take care of these occurrences, and you haven't, so I will. Take me home!"

As we wait for the valet, to my amazement, Katia is still outside. I am so angered at the sight of her, I don't know what to do, or think. I stare at the carryout container in my hands before making a judgment call. Do I go over to smash my open container of crab and parmesan stuffed mushrooms in her face? Or walk away?

Reluctantly, I choose the latter.

Jamaal stares blankly into my eyes, wanting to say something but unable to find the words. I glare back angrily, knowing exactly what I want to say, but choosing to wait until he drops me off. We drive 20 minutes in silence, no radio, no words, just the sound of the tires on the pavement. Finally, we reach my garage. and I collect my thoughts.

"Listen, Jamaal…" I say sincerely. "I don't want you calling to see me anymore. The situation is getting out of hand, so I'm removing myself from it."

"Franchesca! I'm doing my best, but she just won't stop!"

"Have you sought a restraining order? Have you been stern with her? Have you even once called the police?"

He drops his head in personal disappointment. Followed by silence once again.

"I didn't think so. That means that your best isn't good enough. You either secretly enjoy the drama, or you emotionally haven't moved on from her. Either way is good enough for me. Goodbye Jamaal."

Removing myself from the Audi, I proceed to the lobby of my building, excited once again to be inside my condo. Enjoying my nightly gaze upon the city, staring at all the lights on the street, I realize Jamaal hadn't left yet. I wait for ten minutes, hoping he'll leave, but he continues to sit in the driver's seat.

What is he doing? No answer emerges, and I can no longer watch. I retreat from the window, jump into my pajamas and retire in front of the television as my phone rings. Glancing at the screen, it's, again, a number I don't recognize. I silence it, placing it face down on the sofa, while I find

64

something to rest my mind from today's frustration.

***

As the summer winds down, fall is approaching. It has always been my favorite season. The air is crisp, and you can see the elements of nature transform, but best of all, my wardrobe always needs updating! Plus, shopping will give me something to keep my mind off that horrible night, a few weeks ago.

Driving to the mall, I notice a small, folded piece of paper under my windshield wiper. *What is this? Another advertisement?* When I arrive at the mall, I open it.

> *Franchesca, I know you are upset with me*
> *and asked me not to call, so I wrote you a letter.*
> *I know we started off completely wrong, and the*
> *problem is, you think I'm not man enough to handle*
> *my issues or you think I have some attachment to Katia.*
> *But the truth is, you are the only woman I want in my life.*
> *Although, we haven't known each other long, I know I*
> *want to be with you. By the time you read*
> *this and thought to respond, I will have already filed*
> *a restraining order against Katia. I feel it's the best for*
> *us. I hope this touches you enough to reach out to me for a fresh start.*

> *Jamaal*

If he thought this letter would move me, he thought wrong. I've made my decision and it's a bit late. Besides, I shouldn't have to tell a grown man how to handle his business. Had I not approached the situation as an issue, he would've done nothing. Moments after reading the letter, my phone rings.

"Hello?"

"Hi Franchesca, it's Kaleb."

"Oh wow! I haven't heard from you in weeks. What a surprise!"

"I know. I'm out of town trying to settle a family feud. It's a long story."

"Everything's okay, I hope?"

"Much better *now,* thanks. I was calling to see if you wanted to hang out again. Maybe we could go bowling and have pizza."

Bowling? Do people still do that? I mean… It's not the worst idea. I've *actually* had someone ask to take me out to McDonald's from the driver's seat of their car. Of course, I declined. Then he made a follow-up offer to Wendy's. As if that's any better.

"Let me take you bowling. I promise I'll show you a good time."

Blithe's voice travels from the back of my mind, telling me to release my inhibitions and allow myself to have a good time. To maybe ignore that shattered voice inside of me evoking fight or flight. All signs point to a sense of normalcy that I've been unfamiliar with for quite some time, but do I dare step outside of my comfort? Doing so invites the very real possibility of disappointment and that's not a reality I like to live in. I don't think I know how to be in a relationship of any kind anymore. Having the same, one friend for the last four years has kept me cozy like a heated blanket, but just maybe I can stick my foot out.

"I guess we can go out as friends. Sure. But let's make it horseback riding. There's something about transferred shoe funk that doesn't sit right with me."

"Deal!"

67

Chapter 5
Jealousy Unraveled

The ranch is beautiful! It reminds me of the place my aunt used to take me as a kid. There are three acres of open pasture with seven-foot wooden fences painted sky blue. The barn was the same color. You couldn't miss it from the highway. Big and beautiful, like a three-story country home, all to house the horses. I'm more captivated by that, than by the fact a guy actually bringing me here. I love horses! Although I never grew up near any, I've always wanted one. So, to have a man create this scenario on his own is divine. As priceless as the thought is, I can't allow this anomaly to sway my feelings.

Helping me onto the 7-foot stallion is Kaleb, with a smile. Not just any smile, a beaming smile that proves his hoisting me by the rear is not so innocent. I safely plant on my horse and take off riding through the trees. It's wonderful! The wind brushing my skin and the frolic of the horse makes me feel like I'm in a childlike dream!

I almost forgot Kaleb is beside me, until I glance to the right with my heart beating from adrenaline and his chest captivates me. It's as if he was riding in slow motion. Kaleb's body is statuesque, moving his broad shoulders up and down while handling the reigns like a professional. He continues in slow motion as my mind races. I want him right here on top of this beautiful beast! *What am I thinking?* I seem to be asking myself that a lot lately. *Do I have a problem? Nah.* What healthy young woman doesn't crave intimacy from strangers never to be seen again? But Kaleb is a different kind of stranger. Sleeping with him would become too complicated as he wants more than I'm willing to offer. My deciding to just be friends was a hard enough decision. I need to find someone else. He can't be that guy.

After riding for about 10 minutes, we stop by a stream to share a few seconds of silence…

"I figured we'd stop for a while and let the horses get a drink."

"Sure, I could use a break. This saddle is creating some bunching in a couple of crevices," I joked.

"Maybe it's the wrong saddle for you!" He laughs.

"You look like a pro. This can't be your first time riding."

"It isn't. My parents passed this place down to me after they retired. I love riding. It's a good stress relief. Some guys go to the shooting range. I ride horses! Growing up, there was literally not one boy training to be an equestrian. They just pretended to be cowboys."

"I take it you know this from experience. Is this your date spot? What's next? Are you going to bring out the wine, fine cheese, a blanket and start feeding me grapes? Where's the violinist?" I look around the pasture, searching for one.

"Ha ha, very funny!"

This is another great day spent with Kaleb! It's easy to have a good time and not care about what would happen. His phone rings. Remembering a client scheduled to ride today, we head back to the stable. Having a client on the same day as our outing seems odd, but I decide to roll with it. We enter the stable, and I hear a voice that sounds familiar. As I ride the horse closer, I see his face.

"Franchesca?" he says, surprised.

My eyes widen.

"Jamaal? What are you doing here? Are you following me like your psycho ex-girlfriend?!"

He chuckles, but before he can answer, Kaleb re-enters with a horse for Jamaal. "Here she is, your pride and joy. She's been washed, brushed, and she's ready to go!"

Pride and joy? If that horse only knew what she was getting into.

"Franchesca, let me introduce you to Jamaal. One of the best jockey's here in Boston!"

"The *best?* How is it I've never heard of you?"

It's not like I go to horse races. They over-work the animals, spank them for speed and drain them of energy and youth. I'd rather watch the horses be finessed and displayed proudly.

"Maybe our interests are just different in that arena." Gliding his hands across the back of his horse.

I casually shoot him a smile and instruct my horse to turn away from Jamaal and Kaleb by tugging on her reigns, and she gallops into the field where I wait for Kaleb's return. I feel somehow guilty for leading Kaleb to believe I had no idea who Jamaal was, but after all, that's my business to share. Finally, he joins me and we continue to ride. Once again, a seemingly perfect day!

***

Four hours of riding have me ready to retire for the evening. My butt and thighs are sore, so I'm ready for a hot bath. I walk into my bedroom and notice the red blinking light on my answering machine. I press the button.

Hey Franchesca, It's Jamaal. It was a surprise to see you today.
Let's meet up soon. I miss you.

His voice sounds a bit sad, but disguised by pleasantries. He should be upset, but that no longer matters to me. Actually, his feelings never mattered to me… *Delete.*

Second message...

Hey, It's me again... Jamaal. I... um... wanted to clarify
that I wanted to see you sooner than later. Maybe this
week if you aren't too busy. Call me. Bye.

Third message...

I wasn't sure if you still had my number.
It's 371-5827. Call me if you're interested in a date on
Thursday night.

The phone clicks, ending the call after the last message. I stand staring at the machine, wondering why Jamaal would think I would go on another date with him after the last encounter. Wondering why he left three voice messages. Wondering why he called after I told him not to. Part of me wants to call to give him closure to the future that would never be. But, the other part, has no desire to speak with him at all. Wine always helps me think, so I pour myself a glass of Yellowtail Moscato. I sit, I drink and I think… then I make the call.

The phone rings once on my end before he excitedly answers…

"Franchesca! I'm glad you're calling. I didn't think I would hear from you!"

"Hi," I say dryly. "I'm only calling out of courtesy and to not leave you in limbo about this relationship or lack thereof."

"What do you mean?"

"I *mean,* I *wasn't* and *still* am not looking for a serious relationship. I *am* looking for someone to have a good time with, and I chose you. However, the events in your life don't say fun. It exudes drama, so I have to let you go."

"But, we do have fun together," he responds desperately.

71

"Yeah, we do, but your third-party partnership with Katia ruins every moment. Think of this as a lesson. Before you can move on with any woman, you need to clean up the mess with the last one. Until you do that, I won't be the first woman to let you go."

"Listen Franchesca, we were brought together for a reason and we enjoy each other. As for my past—"

I interrupt. I can't bear to listen to him conjure up a scenario about us that wouldn't be true for me. The excuses are too much, and I don't want to hear them. I don't want to fall for what seems like another façade of sensitivity.

"JAMAAL! Raising my voice. "We were *not* brought together for a reason. I sought you out that night because I wanted you in my bed. Nothing else. You seemed fun, and domineering, and I wanted to experience that intimacy. Now, it has turned into something else." *It's a surprise to me that you are still around.*

"Is this what you want? Just to go to bed with me?! He shouts.

"YES!" I flail my arms.

Maybe he finally understands...

"If that's what you want, then that's what you'll get. I'm coming over."

"What? Wait! NO!"

But the call disconnects. Part of the conversation was a turn-on. An anger-induced turn-on. I've never been aroused by anger before. I lay on the sofa with my drink, pondering the thoughts circulating in Jamaal's head. Wondering if he's actually coming over without an invitation.
I hope not.

Half an hour later, I hear faint whispers outside my door. I quietly strain to listen, but the words are distorted. I turn off the television and remove my tipsy body off the sofa to look through the peephole. Before I have the opportunity to get close to the door, a man's abrupt shout startles me.

"FRANCHESCA! IT'S JAMAAL. GET OUT OF THE WAY OF THE DOOR!"
What?

Ignoring the warning, I slowly walk closer. Before I know what's happening my door flies open. Its only savior is the top hinge, which was just replaced a few weeks back. It refuses to disconnect from the frame when he kicks it open like a violent burglar. I stand still, unable to move or speak from bewilderment and fear. My eyes widen. I stare into Jamaal's face as if blinking is no longer a normal human reaction. His face is red, accompanied by fearless emotion. Jamaal walks slowly toward me, speaking to me in a faint whisper, leaving the door barely on its hinges. My body trembles as I leisurely step backward on my left set of toes, slowly lowering my heel to the floor with my right foot following suit.

"You want to have *fun*? You want me for *one reason*, huh?! I'll give you the most amazing one. I don't plan to hurt you, but you brought this on yourself."

He reaches out his hand, rubs his fingers through my hair, and suddenly kisses me hard on the lips. I don't know what to do. I'm still stunned by the events taking place. Removing his hand from my hair, it travels up my back and underneath my button-up blouse.

What is he trying to do? Even with that thought, I remain still because his tender touch relaxes me. His soft, strong hands against my skin turn into a goose-bump-filled moment as shivers run through me. I can't deny him, nor do I want to in these last few seconds. I'm no longer terrified, more like electrified.

Jamaal steps back to view me standing before him, only to undo my blouse, button by button. I stay silent, but we both know that *I* am *his* victim now.

"Is *this* how you hoped things would be between us?" he inquires.

I open my mouth to speak, but there are no words.

Time flies by, entangled in each other's arms. Rolling around on my long hair carpet, experiencing more passion than I had my entire life. New emotions surface that I never knew existed. *But I could keep them at bay?* Looking up from the floor, the realization strikes that the door is still open on its' hinge. There's an audience of my neighbors murmuring, checking to see if I'm okay from the earlier commotion. I'm too enamored with Jammal's comfort to care.

Then I see my ex-fiancé Xander peeking through the crowd. My body clenches at the sight of him, startled by the existence of his face in my doorway. A plethora of emotions surge through me, but there is only one I can effortlessly assign to Xander.

Anger.

The neighbors flee once they notice my glare, but Xander remains, for only a moment. His eyes lower as he fades into the hallway. I listen to Xander's footsteps until Jamaal's words steal my attention.

"If the physical is what you want from our relationship, I can give you that."

"That's *all* I want."

I return to a state of comfort and calm, knowing that Jamaal and I have an understanding. We lay with each other for a little while longer. Jamaal is completely unaware of the events that just took place. Meanwhile, my head is filled with only that.

"We should do this again sometime." He jokes, "And I'll pay for the door."

"Did you think you were going to kick my door in and *not* pay for it?"

Jamaal dresses and leaves me with a kiss. I call Blithe to tell her about my eventful day, and she answers on the first ring.

"Chesca! Guess who just called me?"

Sighing at the thought of playing guessing games. "I don't know Blithe... who?"

"Xander... Xander called me sobbing and pissed off about how he saw you with another guy."

"Seriously? He called you for *that*? What a joke."

How dare he go crying to *my* best friend after what he did? After all this time.

"How the hell did that even happen?"

"I'll just say it was an unfortunate incident that ended not so unfortunately. What was he doing at my place anyway?"

That is the question of all questions.

"He called and said something about wanting to rekindle your relationship. I called your cell and left a message as a heads up."

"Oh well, it serves him right! He cheated on me, started rekindling a relationship with that ex of his and was too much of a coward to let me now about it. I just found out about it one day. I'm glad he saw me and I hope he never forgets. Let's talk later–. I need to get ready for tomorrow. I'm having breakfast with Kaleb and meeting Jamaal after that."

"Wait! Are you fooling with both of them?"

"*NO!* Kaleb is just a *friend*. You and I had this conversation. I don't need two of them chasing me around."

"So, if you just had an anti-relationship talk with Jamaal, why are you sleeping with him and not Kaleb?"

"Oh, that's easy! Because that conversation ended with a hot, angry, paralyzing experience that I couldn't say no to. But Jamaal understands now."

"But Kaleb could understand that too."

She's right. Kaleb might understand, but this is the same guy who asked to take me out weeks before he'd even be back in the state. That doesn't sound like the behavior of a guy looking for something casual. Then again, Jamaal was persistent in getting my attention, even after I cut him off like a bad fingernail.

"I don't know, Blithe. I just can't trust it."

"I'm starting to question your judgement. I'm concerned that your promiscuity is at the precipice of getting out of control. You aren't going to find real love that way."

"I don't want real love. Haven't you been listening to anything I've been saying?" I tilt my head back in frustration.

"Ok, fine. But you're getting something from all these interactions, and it's not just a climax. You're trying to fill a hole, a void, with one-night stands. At this point, I'm just happy you're not accepting money."

I can't believe she just said that. "WOW… THAT'S NOT OK!"

"YOU'RE NOT OK!"

That's when I press the end call button. I can't take her trying to tell me how to live my life. Little *miss perfect* everything. I'm happy that her life is how it is, but mine isn't. Why is this hard for her to just accept my life for what it is? I have.

***

After a not-so-great night, I wake up feeling refreshed and start preparing for breakfast with Kaleb. October has been a warm month so far, so I'll embrace it and wear my flannel mini skirt. As I'm getting dressed, I hear a knock at the door. It must be Kaleb.

"Hey there, beautiful! Are you ready?"

"Let's go. We should go to the new breakfast buffet so I can eat everything. I'm starving."

We drive for 15 minutes before arriving at the buffet. Kaleb sits down, and I immediately head for the waffle station, piling my plate with sausage, bacon, hash browns, and everything I think I can eat.

"Wow, you *are* hungry."

"I told you I wanted to eat everything, and I will finish every last crumb."

"Where are you going to put all this food?"

"It's going straight to my butt!" I turn around to show off my asset.

We both laugh at my indifference to how much food I'm going to inhale as we walk back to the table.

"What did you do with the rest of your evening after horseback riding?"

"I had a friend over for a bit, and the unpleasant surprise of my ex-fiancé showing up. Had a fight with my best friend, so, it was uneventful," I say sarcastically. "How was yours?"

"I actually stopped by last night to drop off a little something for you, but there was such a commotion on your floor I couldn't get through the hallway, so I left. Do you know what was going on?"

"Um… No. I guess it was while I was out." My heart pounds at the idea of Kaleb seeing me in a compromising position.

"It was so weird because it was so quiet for there to be so many people. They were watching something, and I wished I could get through to see what it was. Oh well, here is the little something I have for you."

He reaches over the table to present me with a yellow gift bag covered in fireworks. My eyebrows lift, readying myself for what possibly could be inside. I wrap my hand around the handle, place the bag on my lap and apprehensively peek inside. It's a rectangular grey box wrapped in a silver bow.

"Well, open it," he demands.

After a long inhale, I remove the box from the bag and unwrap the box.

"It's the pendant I've wanting. Wow, It's beautiful!"

I had been looking at this pendant for a couple months, deciding if I really needed another one. I have 12 of them, but this one is the epitome of beauty! It's the shape of a building I had the pleasure of designing a year ago. I'm sure it's not the same, but it looks very similar. Filled with diamonds and amethyst that sparkle amazingly!

I pause. I don't know how to accept this. We're just friends, and we just met five months ago. Is this a gift saying, "Hey buddy, just because you're you," with a wink and finger gun connotation? Or is it saying, "Hey girl, I want to make you mine?"

Should I ask? Or say thank you and move on?

"Well, put it on," he encourages.

I exhale deeply. "Why did you buy this for me?"

"Simply because you wanted it. I remembered you talking about it on various occasions, but you hadn't made the time to go across town to get it. I was hoping you hadn't bought it for yourself already."

"Kaleb, friends don't buy friends extravagant gifts. This is a $300 pendant."

"I know we're just friends, and I appreciate that, but I can afford $300. I own a bar, remember."

"Well, I guess all I can say is thank you! Thank you for thinking of me."

Maybe I *am* overthinking this situation between Kaleb and me. He seems genuine. Plus, I buy Blithe nice gifts all the time. Her recent birthday cost me a nice chunk of change, and I definitely don't want to date her.

"Now that we're done with the crazy talk, are you done with that mountain of food so we can go to a place where there's good coffee? I know the perfect place we can walk to."

We start our short walk to the café, but as Kaleb opens the door for me, I hear someone calling my name. I turn to see who it is.

It's Jamaal.

I quickly slide my hand across my forehead in slight annoyance. *This guy is everywhere.* As often as I see him, he might as well just move in with me. And we *all* know how I'd feel about that.

"What are you doing here? That's three times in two days."

I've been asking him that a lot lately. I guess my life is just one big bubble of uncertainty.

"I was on my way to grab a cup of coffee, and here you are with *Kaleb.* You're just grabbing coffee with your horse-riding instructor? Are you on a date?"

"NO!" I roll my eyes. "Just two friends out for coffee."

"And Kaleb, how have you been since I saw you last? I didn't know you and Franchesca were such good friends."

"I didn't know you and Franchesca were friends, either. Small world!"

They both turn to me as if they're expecting an explanation. Which I will not be giving. I turn away and begin to walk into the café and they both follow. And Jamaal continues to be passive-aggressive as I make a B-line for the counter to order my coffee. Starting to feel uneasy about the situation, I consider asking Kaleb if he wants to take a walk with our coffee instead of dining in. I'm hoping he says yes, so we can leave immediately. But before I can utter the words, Jamaal ends his conversation with Kaleb and turns to me.

"Franchesca, may I have a word with you?"

I reluctantly submit to his request. He guides me around the corner out of sight, next to the restrooms, and gently presses my back against the wall. He kisses me passionately, pulling me closer by the back of my neck with one hand, while the other is wrapped securely around my back. I don't stop him; the intensity of being in public makes me want him more.

Then, he whispers,

"I thought you chose me? I thought we chose each other?" Walking his fingers up my left shoulder.

"What are you talking about? I thought we had an understanding. We are only 2am buddies."

"— For each other, only. But here you are with Kaleb."

"It's not 2am, and Kaleb and I are *just* friends, —with no benefits."

How is he this jealous? We slept together once. If Jamaal is going to be *this* possessive, maybe we should call it quits. This is not what I signed up for.

He grabs my hand and guides me to the single-stall women's restroom. We enter and lock the door.

He runs both hands through my hair, and smashes his lips to mine. We exchange deep breaths as his lips travel to my decolletage. I allow my body to lean into his seduction. Two years ago, I never would've considered the idea, but here I am, unable to say no. Not wanting to say no.

Unable to say no to the deed? Or to him?

Blithe could be right, but I don't have time to think about that right now. The pleasure of my flesh has consumed me.

Several moments pass, and I realize I've been absent for an amount of time that could raise questions with Kaleb, so I reluctantly cut our session short, and retreat to my coffee.

"Is everything okay Franchesca?"

"Everything's great." I sigh. "Jamaal and I have somewhat of a past that we needed to talk through." Hoping that's the first and last question he'll ask about my absence.

"Oh. I didn't know you two knew each other. At the ranch, it seemed like you two were strangers."

"I didn't want to spend time catching up with him while I was hanging out with you."

I see Jamaal resurface from the corner, but I try not to offer eye contact. He walks to the counter to place the to-go order for his coffee, and once the order is complete, he walks to me and whispers once more.

"This is what *you* asked for."

I smile coyly and want him all over again. I can't help myself... and he's right. After these last couple of encounters, I'm not sure if I want to seek out anyone else. I've never had the experiences I'm having with Jamaal with anyone else.

It's addicting, but which part? I truly have become his victim.

Chapter 6

The Victim

I haven't heard from Kaleb in about a month. Maybe our last encounter with Jamaal led him to believe there's something more than what I was letting on. He'd be right, but I'll never tell. Kaleb has been a good friend, but in my soul, I think he's hoping for something more. Maybe we could've been if I'd met him back in college. But I don't want him to waste his time on me, especially if he could find someone right now.

I'm happy with the way things have been so far, even though I've *only* been with Jamaal. My mind is constantly veering toward the fantasy of him. The way his shoulders broaden when he walks toward me, his chest standing at attention. It's masculinity at its' finest. But in the midst of all this, I can't help but think, *where's the Franchesca who prowls the bar at night?* What happened to never seeing the same guy twice? At what point did I break the solidarity between my body and my mind to end up here?

What happened?

Every other day is filled with Jamaal's presence. Almost as if he's made me part of his routine. Visits to my office for lunchtime excursions and to my place for after-work rendezvous. He's done a complete 180. Instead of trying to date me, he seems to have welcomed the idea of only having a physical relationship, and it's been carnal euphoria! Jamaal has taken me over. I'll do whatever he wants me to, but in the end, it will be a sad day for him when I have to cut the strings.

A couple of weeks ago, Jamaal thought it would be a great idea for us to go on a road trip. Since I have a ridiculous amount of vacation time, I agreed. Although I wasn't looking forward to the 18-hour drive it takes to get there. Who drives to Florida from Massachusetts? Being stuck in the car, eating fast food, and stopping at messy roadside bathrooms is not my idea of a good time. The last time I went on a road trip, Xander and I got lost. We argued the entire time and ended up staying overnight at a trailer park disguised as a campground haunted attraction. So, one can imagine my thoughts on future road trips after that, but Jamaal insisted.

Shoving the last of my belongings inside my Dooney & Burke overnight bag, I head for the door when my cell phone rings…

"Hi, my beautiful girlfri— girl." Jamaal corrects. "Your chariot awaits!"

"I'll be right down."

I open the door to rush downstairs, and there he is, waiting right outside of it. He sweeps me and my bag off the floor as if we weigh nothing at all. *Is this what it feels like to be swept off your feet? Startled and uncomfortable.* He walks toward the elevator, me and my bag still in his arms.

81

"Put me down." I flail like a toddler.

"Never. I have a surprise for you." He smirks.

"If you drop me, you're going to wish you had used these muscles for something else."

"I'd never drop a precious gem."

I squint with curiosity as my mouth curls to one side and release a slight groan as the elevator doors open. We enter, and a neighbor takes a step to follow, but Jamaal's words bring him to a halt.

"Excuse me, sir. You might want to take the next one, if you know what I mean," He says, offering a wink and a smile.

My neighbor quickly steps off the elevator, allowing the door to close. Immediately after, my mouth opens, and hysterical laughter comes over me.

"What are you laughing at?"

"You, telling that man he couldn't get on. Who are you? Elevator security?"

"Don't laugh. I want you to myself for the next 20 floors."

Jamaal pushes the lobby button as my back rests in the corner of the elevator and his lips find mind. And the countdown begins…

Once we arrive in the lobby, he carries me and my luggage to the car. He plants me in the front passenger seat, buckles my belt, and we begin to ride. The road trip starts smoothly with a bit of Lenny Kravitz on the radio until I plug in the USB to my phone. I can tell Jamaal is taken back when Hideaway by Kiesza starts to play. You can't have a road trip without pop culture! After being on the road for half a day with music, naps and bathroom breaks, Jamaal exhales a sigh. His mouth opens, and a slew of probing questions eject in rapid fire.

"So, what's your story? I mean, why don't you want a boyfriend? Did something happen?"

My eyes travel in a half circle from left to right in aggravation. *When is the road part of this trip going to be over?* We haven't been in a situation where we needed to talk to each other for very long and never about something so personal. Talking about my ex brings up old feelings I'd rather keep buried.

"I don't have a boyfriend because I don't want one."

"But why?"

"Because I'm not obligated to have one," I snap.

"I'm just trying to understand you. Get to know you as a person. I like you."

"How can you like me when you barely know me?" I stare daggers into the side of his face from

82

the passenger seat, waiting for a logical response. "You CAN'T! And that's the point."

He tightens his grip on the steering wheel, refusing to offer a retort, his eyes wide open, glaring at the two-lane highway in front of us. The top row of teeth bites into his bottom lip like a vice grip. He seems angry. I'm sure Jamaal will come to his senses and turn this car around, but he doesn't. *Should I say or do something to ease the tension?* No. Instead, I gaze out the passenger window, keeping my attention on passersby for miles, until we stop for food and gas. I see the green marker sign; Welcome to the City of Savannah. *Only three more hours to go.*

Finally, we reach Palm Coast. I roll down the window and let the breeze blow through my hair. The warm gusts are refreshing and coastal. A nice break from the chill of Boston's November air. I still have no idea what Jamaal has planned for us, but hopefully, we can salvage it after our last episode. Whatever it is, will it be worth it?

Pulling into the hotel parking lot, I'm filled with joy at the sight of a 50-foot palm tree swaying gracefully in the wind. Feeling the moist air on my skin has me longing for the beach. I could already feel the crumbs of soft sand between my toes. Jamaal grabs the bags and escorts me by the elbow to the check-in counter, interrupting my vivid daydream. We retrieve the key cards; he hits me on the shoulder with his hand and runs to the elevator.

"You're it!"

Good to know he's back to being himself because I need him. If I were on this trip alone, I would find some unsuspecting vacationer to fulfill my desires. But there's something about Jamaal that allows me to relinquish myself to him and abandon my self-control. Traveling up the elevator with him makes me remember the last time we were in one. The thought makes me weak in the knees. *How can someone you barely know make you feeble in mind and body?*

Entering the hotel room, I don't know what I expected. Maybe some rose petals on the bed or a bottle of chilled champagne awaiting us. Afterall, what guy books a vacation with a woman and doesn't plan to stay in the room for most of it? Instead, it's a standard hotel room. Two beds, a TV, a mini fridge, and a window that barely opens. But it does have a scent of florals. A combination of roses, honey, and fresh linens. Filled with the intoxicating aroma, I lie on the bed, close my eyes, and soak it all in.

"We have somewhere to be. Grab your suit." He rushes me.

"We have two whole days. Don't you want to hang around the hotel for awhile?"

"There's today and tomorrow before we head back. Besides, we didn't come all this way to stay in the room the entire time, silly."

What does he mean we aren't staying in the room? Well, I can't be too upset. It's not like we aren't going to come back to it later. Perhaps tomorrow I'll get my wish. He's right. Driving all those grueling hours to take advantage of my time off would be a waste if we stayed inside. Finally, being able to take a vacation is heavenly in itself, but spend time with someone I enjoy is also refreshing. I don't know him well, but he's pleasant, kind, and has no strings attached. Although, I often wonder if this will have to come to an end. Maybe he will meet someone offering more than I'm willing to give him. My fear is that one day I will actually grow to like him and be forced to end a good thing. Being hurt once is enough. Letting someone get close enough to steal my heart just to run away with it will never happen again. So, I'll revel in these moments for as long as possible.

After showering 18 hours of travel dust and confinement funk off myself, we pack our bathing suits and jump in the car again for another ride. A 45-minutes' drive to the beautiful Blind Creek Beach. We walk to the middle of the beach to find a spot; I begin to notice something unusual. No children in sight building sandcastles or audibly expressing excitement or splashing about. And most of the land is isolated.

"Where are you taking me?" I ask puzzled.

Jamaal turns to me and responds with only a smile, then pulls me closer as we walk inside.

"Look around 'Chesca. Where do you think we are?"

I pan the landscape with intense curiosity and finally realize that almost everyone is naked.

"A NUDE BEACH! You took me to a nude beach!?" My shock turns to intrigue.

"I thought it would be something you and I could enjoy for the first time. I told you it would be invigorating!"

"Yeah, you did say that, but this is weird."

My heart is racing, and every sense seems to amplify. I inhale nothing except the salt of the ocean and medicated sunscreen. Sweat beads just under my hairline and down my back. My eyes quickly shift from side to side to avoid the view of naked bodies everywhere until a woman jogging the shoreline fixes my sight. Every fleshy part of her being undulates against her body with every step. The wave-like motion of her curves makes it seem like she's running in slow motion. Seeing her in this moment, makes me feel like I could do this. My heartrate slows. I stand tall with my chin up and place both hands on my hips as if I have transformed into an empowered superhero.

I can do this!

We set up the chairs and cooler for much-needed relaxation. Sitting with my cocktail, gazing into the ocean, I almost forget I'm surrounded by hundreds of naked bodies. Until I see Jamaal escaping from his swim trunks, bearing himself for all to see. With my new-found inspiration, I join him. Jamaal stares at me as if seeing me for the first time. His eyes travel from my face to my midsection as I break my posture to sit in my lounge chair. Twirling the curls of my hair, I turn my head toward him, and he quickly looks away as if I caught him doing something wrong.

"What?" I inquire.

He rubs the back of his neck nervously. "Nothing. I just… don't want to look."

"Okaaay."

What does he mean he doesn't want to look? I glare at him through my sunglasses, hoping for a revised response, but it doesn't come. My forehead wrinkles downward into my eyebrows with confusion, wanting to ask more questions. But I decide to let it go.

As the hours pass, I become more comfortable with the idea of being exposed and having Jamaal with me makes it easier. He seems to make most things effortless. Well, everything except talking. I wake up happier knowing I might see him for a rendezvous that day. Going to bed is more voluntary after he *tucks* me in at night. Nothing and no one else matters when we're together, but that connection is only sustainable when we're physically intertwined. The emotions are sensationally overwhelming in those moments. Making me crave it all the time. Simple activities effortlessly turn erotic in my mind. I *need it.* I *need him.*

I sprint out of the lounge chair, grab his hand and drag him to the ocean until the water is chest deep. Standing face to face, holding hands, listening to the seagulls speak their love language. Waves crashing against us, hardly able to keep our footing. This is my chance to gain control and take what's been owed to me.

"Are you ready?" I ask.

"For what?"

I leap onto him with my left arm around his neck and both legs around his waist. I'm sure he thinks that will be the end of it, but this is only the beginning.

"Right here, right now."

"Franchesca, no."

I continue to try to take what is mine. What he's always been willing to give. I pull him in with the seductive prowess, which I almost forgot I have, but Jamaal leans backward and away from my attempt.

"Frachesca, what are you doing?"

"What we always do. What you started." I continue trying to entice him.

Pulling away for the second time. "No. I don't want this." Shaking his head.

"We can always go back to the hotel." I smile.

Jamaal takes both hands, grabs me just beneath my armpits on each side and throws me backward into the ocean. After inhaling a bit of water, I resurface, and frustration comes over me.

"WHAT'S YOUR PROBLEM!"

"*My* Problem?!" Looking around as if he's checking for an audience, then proceeds to lower his voice. "Look at yourself. I don't want to fool around out here, and your response to that is trying to do it anyway?"

"How dare you? You offer yourself to me on a whim, I'm literally at your mercy and you choose *now* to revoke my access?" I yell.

"The difference is, that's what *you* wanted, AND *you've* never said no." He points at me. "I never wanted this! I kicked your door in because I was angry and wanted to show you I could be *that* guy. I let my ego get the best of me, but I can't keep up with the charade. I want you Franchesca, but not like this."

I stand in the water, soaking wet, watching as he wades through the waves back to the sand, and it gives me pause. How had this become a double standard? What's good for the goose, should be good for the gander, right?! I'm confused... and maybe a bit stupid. Before I pulled him into the ocean, my mind told me maybe that wasn't a good idea, but my desires spoke louder than my thoughts. So, I tried... and failed. I quiver at the thought of him weakening me with his touch. *How could he say no? And more importantly, did he really want to?* Jamaal had me in his clutches and seemingly wasn't letting go... until today. He victimized me in the best and the worse ways, and now, I don't know what to do.

87

Chapter 7

Back on the Bandwagon

I almost feel guilty for leaving Jamaal in Florida like a thief in the night. But I didn't think I had another choice. I've become addicted to him, and he won't let me have my fix. Staying any longer would give him a false sense of reality, and I don't want to confuse him. Or myself. I don't understand why he would suddenly bring me on a weekend trip to show disinterest. I didn't know how to feel about this shift, but I knew I couldn't spend one more day around his half-clothed physique and not have permission to devour it. I felt like I no longer fit into the bubble we created.

I text him a screenshot of my boarding pass, so he wouldn't think I was adult-napped or something. Immediately after, my cell lit up like a Christmas tree for exactly five calls, but I couldn't bring myself to answer. *What could he possibly say to me?* Because I didn't have one word to share. Maybe what we had has run its' course, and it's time to move on. But I had plenty of time on the flight back to Boston to think about it.

It's been roughly a week since my Floridian escape. The more time that passes, the more my mind becomes more disoriented in what I want and need versus what's right and wrong. There's so much noise in my head, I can't think logically. I want to move on, but my thoughts seem to be magnetized to him. Pacing the living room carpet, like a teenager trying to clean up a party before their parents get home. My perception is a mess and there's nothing I can do about it.

Screw it!

I get dressed, grab my trench coat, and barrel down the hall to the elevator. Logic isn't guiding me tonight. It's pure desire! Desire is easy. There's no *process* behind desire. It's just your flesh needing what it wants, and you give in to it. You embrace the guilty pleasure until it beckons you once again.

Speeding from the parking garage, blasting a playlist that entices my sultry confidence! Lip-syncing to every word. *My milkshake brings all the boys to the yard—*

Seconds feel like minutes, until the GPS confirms my arrival. I screech into the driveway. Quickly exiting the car, I drop my keys. As I pick them up, I exhale slowly through pursed lips and casually glide to the front door. I knock, and a guy I don't recognize opens the door, beer in hand.

Raising my eyebrows. I say, "I'm looking for Jamaal."

The discovery I make when walking into Jamaal's place feels like someone tore through my chest and squeezed all the emotion from my heart. I can't breathe. Hoping for some semblance that this exposed reality is just my subconscious and I'll wake up wrapped in my duvet. I'd love a good joke right now, but unfortunately, it seems the joke is on me while Jamaal just stands in the doorway.

How could he not say one word as I ran out the door?

I sit in my car in Jamaal's driveway for what seems like an eternity. The tears build behind my eyes. I want to scream. Instead, I clench both hands into fists and beat every surface within reach. The passenger seat, the steering wheel, even the radio, as an unwanted love song begins to play. *Okay, Mariah, clearly, we don't belong together.*

Just as my fury grows hotter, an un-named number rings my cell. *It's the same area code as the times before.* I pick up the phone, bring it to my chest, and gaze into its' brightness, as if the remedy to my anger is going to appear. Moments that feel like an eternity has passed. Still peering at the screen as it goes dark and the ringtone silences. I lift my eyes, and at that moment, I see someone peek through the curtain of the house and quickly retract. I realize I've over-stayed my welcome in this man's driveway and lazily toss the phone to the passenger seat. I turn the key and begin my sullen trek of shame.

I knew one day he would find someone who could value him more than I was able to, but I didn't think it would happen two days after our so-called vacation. And now, this all seems so wrong. *How did it not seem wrong before?* Getting involved with him was reckless, and I knew it from the start. Allowing myself to succumb to that type of relationship… with one man, long-term. *How stupid was I?* I take a deep breath, pushing back new tears, realizing I brought this on myself.

I will *not* make this mistake again. I promise.

Arriving home, my anger turns to unexpected sadness while entering the key into the newly replaced door. The telephone rings. The caller ID says it's Blithe. *Do I really feel like talking?*

"Yeah, Blithe?" I say dryly.

"Yeah, to you too. What's going on, 'Chesca? Xander keeps calling. Then texting me, saying you aren't answering your phone."

"What? Why would he be calling me? How am I supposed to kn—" My eyes widen as I slowly release the air from my lungs. "Ooh! Maybe *he's* been the random number that's been calling these past few weeks. Oh well. I'm not interested."

"I know. But he won't stop calling until you talk to him. So, at least just tell Xander to get lost, so he stops calling *me*."

Why is Xander suddenly back in town? But more importantly, why is he trying to get in contact with me after all this time? I hadn't heard his voice since graduation, so as far as I'm concerned, he's dead.

I reluctantly sigh, walking from room to room. "Fine! I hear you."

"You're snippy tonight. What's your problem? Because this thing with Xander can't be it."

"I'm fine." Peeking through my vertical blinds, hoping she'd drop it.

"You know it's unhealthy to bottle up your emotions. It's going to expose itself sooner or later. You could be in a meeting talking about your next project, then BOOM! You're cracking under the pressure, explaining to your team how cement doesn't care about anyone, and that's why it's so strong."

"Okay. Okay. Geez. You're laying it on pretty thick, aren't you?" I release another sigh. "Fine. I decided to surprise Jamaal with a late-night rendezvous. I dressed in nothing except pumps and a trench, but when I arrived, he and another woman appeared from the back of the house. She was still buttoning her dress. I left. I raged. And now I'm okay."

"Well, 'Chesca, it could've been innocent. You don't know what was really going on, only what it looked like."

"She was straightening her clothes, so tell me, Blithe, what does that look like?... I'll wait."

"Ok, fine. It could be what you're thinking it is, but you still aren't 100% sure what happened, regardless of how it looked. But, the more important question is, why are you so upset? You said you were only having fun… no emotional attachment."

"You're right, and he knew that. But at the very least, he could have told me he wanted to move on, and I would've done the same."

"Moved on to who? Kaleb?" Blithe inquires jokingly.

"Maybe." I grab a bag of chips from the pantry.

"No! You already protested luring Kaleb would be nothing short of a bad idea. He's a friend, plus you really should be well satisfied by the recent activities of your lower half. You and Jamaal were going at it so much, I was starting to get jealous, and I'm *married*."

We both laugh, understanding who is right and who is insane, me being the latter.

"Ok Chesca, I'm going to go fiddle with my husband. Please try to use this time to focus on yourself. I'm sure there are more promising activities you can engage in."

"Is that your official prescription?'"

"GOODBYE." Blithe chuckles.

As she disconnects the call, I realize she's right, as she often is. I spend a lot of time finding prey to fulfill my sexual needs, before discarding them. It's become second nature. *So, how am I supposed to stop fulfilling this need with the snap of my fingers? Withhold my insatiable appetite?*

A swirl of sarcastic humor overwhelms my mind. Changing my behavior after all this time seems ridiculous. What if I just stop going to bars altogether and enlist in the nunnery? *That would be terrible.* As crazy as it sounds, I owe it to myself to try to get my mind off Jamaal. Besides, there are plenty of things to do in Boston, and I might find a hobby other than playing with men… Maybe.

After the event with Jamaal, the weekend feels as if it decelerated. More thoughts of him accompanied by more questions. He resides in my brain like an unwanted tumor. It's been a couple days of my phone incessantly ringing. And every time it sounds, I have no reason to believe it isn't Jamaal, so I've been ignoring most of the calls coming in. But, after each call, he leaves a message, and I decide that it's time to listen to all 18 of them. I place my phone on the kitchen counter, press the speaker button, and do some chores as I listen. The first one is Jamaal expounding on what I saw. Or, according to him, what I *think* I saw. My eyes roll carelessly as I casually wash a dirty plate.

After a while of listening to Jamaal, his tone shifts from wallowing in his singleness to blaming me for pushing him away, and I'm thinking of calling it quits. I can't listen to another message, but I realize there's only one more left. A voicemail from today. *Do I even bother?* Nothing he's said so far makes me want to let my guard down or spend more time with him. He was the only one I'd been giving myself to, and he so casually moved on to the next girl. He didn't even give me the courtesy of a heads-up. That shows how much respect he has for me.

Or maybe I need to be an adult, get over it and accept the fact that I was just an insignificant piece of casual excitement for him too. We both shared emotionless, meaningless encounters that were only meant to effervesce in those moments.

So, why does it feel like I'm convincing myself?

The doorbell interrupts the furious rant. Pounding each foot on the hardwood as I make my way to the door. I place my hand on the knob and yank. "WHAT?!"

I sigh at the appearance of no one, only the hallway wall staring back at me. As I attempt to close the door, shielding myself from further embarrassment, I notice a bouquet of lilies.

My favorite!

I pick them up with my mouth agape and search the flowers for a hint of who they're from. When I see the name of the sender, my face tries to force back a smile. *I guess Jamaal is trying a different approach.*

Suddenly, I remember there's one last message to listen to. I press play, and his voice is soft and compassionate this time. Allowing me to lean in to receive what he might say next. Then I hear the sweet sound of an apology murmur in my ear. In that moment, I understand myself a bit more. I want him to care about me even though I struggle to show him reciprocity.

I'm happy this Monday morning when my alarm sounds. I have a long stretch under my duvet and have the realization that I don't have to batter myself about Jamaal.

Sitting at my desk, I begin daydreaming about Jamaal's lips, his masculine hands reaching out for me, the ferocity of our encounters, and how he made me feel. I find myself drifting farther away from my current state into sensual tranquility. It's difficult to stop my thoughts, but I have no choice. Our time was great together, but I can't allow myself to dwell on the past. This weekend will be the time for new opportunities.

***

It's finally here! The part of the week I've been looking forward to. That time I use to unwind. This is how I retrieve my control. Control that Jamaal stole from me. I'm taking back the power ripped from me by every man I've loved and cared for. Men are my prey, and this weekend, I will take some heads!

Trying to find my next victim has become my drug, and I am a fiend. I decide to visit Martini Life Lounge to see if Kaleb is bartending to execute a seamless transition back into my old ways. I grab a seat at the bar, and he is already serving up my drink.

"Apple martini for the pretty lady."

"AHH, you remembered!" I smile.

"Of course, I did! I am a bartender, entrepreneur, and hopeless romantic!"

"So, how have you been stranger?" I ask nonchalantly.

"Pretty good. The bar has been booming since the new year is around the corner. How about you?"

"Nothing too crazy. Although, this week has given a new meaning to 'work like a slave.'"

"Yeah, but you definitely get paid more than one!" He says jokingly.

"That's true, but the feeling is still the same."

"So, how's your love life?"

I almost choke as I take the first sip of my drink. "What?" Looking up from my drink like a surprised doe in headlights. "What makes you think I had one? Why would you even ask?"

"Oh. I'm asking because Jamaal was in here kind of seeking advice on how to handle you."

Handle me? What am I?... An effing bicycle?

"What do you mean handle me?" I ask.

"He just didn't know what to do with your *little* situation, so he was seeking guidance."

"He should be talking to me about that, don't you think?" Inhaling the last two large gulps from my martini glass. "Plus, it's been five days since his floral apology, and I haven't heard from him. I think it's safe to say he's moved on." Flashing a crooked smile that went away just as quickly as it appeared.

"Five days, huh. Look who's counting."

"Just be quiet and give me another drink."

"I didn't mean to bring up a sore subject. I'm just trying to be a friend and let you know that he cares."

"I already know he cares. Or cared. It doesn't matter. We were only messing around anyway, so, it's nothing to seek council over."

As the bar crowd grows, Kaleb relieves his role as bartender to front of the house concierge, leaving me to think about why I'm really here. I search the scene for the next potential guest for my bed. All I can think of is the next pleasurable moment I could have and how soon I will have it! I oversee the crowd by twisting my upper body toward the back of my chair. And try to interpret indistinct conversations, but the music is louder than usual. So, my senses are off. With my second drink in hand, I exit my chair and begin to prowl. My urges are prominent, so exuberant, I can hardly contain myself. I want the touch of a man. I need to feel his embrace. My body shivers for every man in the room watching me. Feeling a warm hand on the small of my back shocks me into stopping my stride, and I gasp for air.

"Hi, I'm Jonathan. I wanted to know if you would like to dance?" he whispers in my ear.

His warm breath sends tingles down my spine.

"Yes… I answer breathlessly.

This is an opportunity to have his warm body against mine. He escorts me to the dance floor, an intimate 9foot x 9foot space, his hand still guiding me from my lower back. I love every second of his touch, and the fire starts to burn within me. As we dance, I feel additional hands caressing me from behind, on my shoulders and the back of my arms. Turning around, I'm surprised by his beauty. His identical beauty.

"This is my twin brother James"

"Hi. I can see that! I'm Franchesca." I smile.

I am happily sandwiched between the two handsome men validating the attention I need. I don't think once about them stopping. The sensation is titillating, and I wouldn't stop if I could. I feel desired. I feel alive! And no one can take that from me. James runs his fingertips up and down my arms as he dances with me, while Jonathan grips both my shoulders, burying his face inside my neck, swaying me side to side from behind. I'm being devoured, and I have no problem being their prey for now. Thoughts of inviting them both home enter my mind, but I know my conscience won't allow it. I turn to Jonathan…

"Would you want to go back to my place?"

"I just got here," he replies.

"That's fine. I could take James if you prefer?"

"Let me just cash out my tab."

***

Jonathan drives his car to my condo, and I can't sit still. The seatbelt starts to feel claustrophobic around me. My hands begin to sweat. It becomes more difficult to control my behavior. I try to keep it together until we arrive at my home, but the temptation is too strong. I release all inhibitions, unfasten my safety belt and jump into the driver's seat.

"What are you doing?!" He raises his voice in surprise.

"Just go with the flow," I respond.

He pulls off the road, and we do just that.

Blithe was wrong. This is the only activity I need.

Chapter 8
The Aftermath

How could I have acted this way? I behaved like a drunken sorority girl. Who's happy about being groped by two men in public and not even bat an eyelash? Instead, I reveled in it, basked in it and adored the sensation. Who *was* that woman? Who have I become? I, Franchesca Veranda, a lady of class, despite my choice of reckless promiscuity, am always in control… ALWAYS! But, last night, my body took over.

I lost control, I lost myself. Who have I become? More importantly, can I stop it?

The doorbell interrupts my thoughts of self-humiliation. Looking through the peephole, I see it's Jonathan. Somehow, I'm excited, but bewildered by the idea of him at my doorstep unannounced. I open the door in my robe.

"What are you doing here?" I ask.

"Well, it's nice to see you again too!" He chuckles. "After all the rush last night, I think my keys were left here last night. There were two sets and I think one is here, so I thought I'd stop by to pick them up."

"Oh, I haven't seen any, but feel free to look around."

As I watch him in his slim denim, tight tee shirt and leather jacket, I crave him all over again. Watching as he bends to search underneath the sofa, I relive the moments of last night. My imagination runs away with me in the backseat, again. Dropping my robe, and revealing my natural self, I walk over while his back is toward me. Reaching my arms around him, resting my face against his shoulder. He jumps and turns to me…

"What are you doing, Franchesca?" Raising his voice.

"What does it look like? I thought we had fun last night." Saying seductively.

"Franchesca… I'm James. You were with Jonathan last night. I'm just here because he couldn't stop by himself to get my keys."

I pause for a moment. Slightly embarrassed by the realization, but the call of my desire is deafening to the murmurs of logic. I walk toward him.

"I'm sorry for the confusion," I whisper.

I reach for him again, only this time, more slowly.

"You're already here. Can't we pretend?" pursing my lips together.

"Franchesca, I have a girlfriend."

"Your girlfriend isn't here and I'm sure you're a good little boy, but let's have an adventure for a short time. Then you can go back to being her knight in shining armor."

Immediately, I grab his face with both hands, kiss him and pull him closer. I take his arms to wrap them around my waist. He allows me to guide him with hesitation, but he succumbs to my prowess. I take him by the hand as an invitation to show him who I need him to be. To be who I wish he was. Only to leave him where I found him afterward. At my doorstep. Tossing him away because he never mattered.

My weekend rendezvous have become my drug. My outlet. My exhilaration and, to some degree, my happiness. I need my power back and I'm willing to do anything to get it. At one point, sex was only casual. A basic need for my human flesh, but now things have changed. Going on the hunt is exuberant! Knowing I can lure any kind, unsuspecting gentleman home with me is the reward. The aftermath is my crown. I will never step foot in another relationship. They don't deserve me, but I'll take what I deserve.

***

I take a walk to my favorite coffee café to clear my mind. As I travel through the corridor of my building, the brisk winter air shivers through me. I bundle up a bit more by gently wrapping my oversized wool scarf around my neck. Placing one foot in front of the other, my boots crunch in the freshly shoveled snow, as I notice the white dusting piling in the leafless trees, shimmering from the delicate radiance of the sun. I Inhale the dampness and nearby coffee in the air. Watching as unknown neighbors walk their fur babies, engaging in comradery and laughter with their companions. This is the first time in a while that I've stepped outside my head to notice the life around me.

Lightly placing my hand on the café's door handle, I give it a slight twist, and the brewed aroma fills my soul. I place my order, sit at the table by the window, continuing to indulge in people-watching. *Is that...? It is.* Kaleb is walking through the crosswalk approaching the café. I shield my face with both hands, hoping he continues to pass the entrance.

Seconds go by and I hear nothing. *Maybe he didn't stop in.* I remove my hands as the barista calls my name to pick up my delicious 20-ounce cup of recovery, happily grabbing it to return to the window of solitude.

"Franchesca?" a voice calls out.

My heart drops. I slowly turn in my seat.

"Franchesca! I'm glad you're here."

So much for the idea of Kaleb not stopping by. I don't have the energy to put on a joyous façade today. I just want to be alone with my thoughts and drink a gallon of coffee. I'm not at the point of adding conversation to the agenda.

"Hey," I respond dryly.

"What's wrong with you?"

"Honestly. I'm not in the mood for human interaction at the moment."

"Oh. Well, maybe you're in the mood for a friend after last night."

What does he know about last night? He sits there judging me silently, but not so subtly.

"Do you have something on your mind?" I ask begrudgingly.

"I've never seen you act like you did last night and I want to be here for you. I want to be the friend you can talk to if you need to. Or the friend you can be with when you don't want to talk. All you have to do is let me in, Franchesca."

I'm guessing he completely misinterpreted what I meant when I said, "No human interaction." I know he means well, and he has been a good friend on the surface. But, letting him penetrate beyond the shell into a meaningful connection... I don't know how I feel about that type of commitment. I have Blithe. She's been part of my soul since we were college roommates, and we've never detached. She's my everything and no one can replace her. Especially not someone I just met a few months ago.

"What are you doing on this side of town? You live in Mission Hill."

"This place has the best coffee. So, the 15-minute drive is worth it."

"You drove all this way, not for the museums, but for the coffee?" I ask skeptically.

He takes a sip, then smacks his lips. "Yup!"

I end the conversation with a chuckle, continue to sip my coffee and stare out the window.

Moments of silence turn into an awkward lull that becomes unbearable until he blurts.

"Let's have a movie day! Snacks, popcorn, relaxation and fun."

"You're not going to let this go, are you?"

"You need me right now."

"*Need* is a strong word. *Need* is synonymous with sustenance, and you are not that... But Fine."

We take our time enjoying our coffee and order another cup. With more caffeine, I open up and become less irritable, realizing the nuances of my and Kaleb's friendship. We enjoy each other's company, I feel comfortable being myself and he doesn't lecture me about my life. Having one friend in my life to mother me, is enough. Suddenly, the idea of a movie day with Kaleb didn't seem like a chore.

Sliding the key into the door lock, I allow Kaleb in first.

"Go ahead. Make yourself at home. Snacks are in the kitchen."

I jump in the shower. Steamy water relaxed me from the chill of the outdoors. Pouring body wash onto the loofah, the smell of candied apples fills my nostrils. I love taking a shower, knowing I have that smell to look forward to, and I hate when it come to an end. Leaving the shower without drying, I grab my sweats, enter the kitchen for a fresh cup of thin mint coffee, and stretch my legs across the sofa next to my buddy.

"Now, *this* is what I call lounging!" I snuggle under my Sherpa throw blanket.

I wiggle my toes to express my giddiness, but Kaleb mistakes it as a nonverbal queue to rub my feet, which I don't resist. I've had plenty of body parts massaged in the last couple of months. None of which were my feet, so it's refreshing. I almost forgot how nice it feels.

"You have lovely feet, Franchesca".

"Those pedicures work wonders when you walk around in Minolos all day. Are you going to pick a movie or what?"

He places my other foot on the sofa, slowly leans toward me, and gently kisses my neck.

"Kaleb, what are you doing?" I lean away from him.
Between kisses, he decides to answer.

"I saw you at the lounge with those two guys. It looked as though you needed some attention."

"You saw me? I wasn't myself last night. It was all very confusing, and it still is."

"You've never let a man touch you, but there were two. I never see you dance, but you were on the dance floor. There was something *very* different about you and whatever it is, I want to cater to it."

"Kaleb, we're friends. I don't want to ruin that!" I protest.

"But you let two strangers get close to you in a way that only someone who cares for you should."

He continues to kiss me. I condone his behavior with my nonverbal willingness, while still trying to talk sense to him, and myself.

"We CAN'T do this! You're looking for a relationship, and I don't want to hurt you."

Several moments of silence allows me too much time to think about the pro's and cons of this situation. But then he whispers…

"I saw you with those two guys last night, and it made me want to make my move on you

102

before another 'Jamaal' came along to take you from me. Seeing you with them, I knew you weren't yourself. I want to be here for you mentally and physically. The physical comes right now because I know that's what you desire. I can stimulate your mental needs later."

I don't know if I should be upset or intrigued. Willing or apprehensive. Kaleb is making it difficult to concentrate on what I should or shouldn't be doing. What I shouldn't be allowing. The one day that I want to get as far away from intimacy as possible is when it gets thrown at me.

How long has he had these feelings about me? All the gifts, the unannounced visits, wanting to know the details of my "relationship" with Jamaal. How could I have been so naive? He's been using our friendship to manipulate me this entire time. Waiting for his moment to pounce.

My heartbeat increases. Thudding so intensely, I think it can be seen through my chest. I stare Kaleb in the face, watching his lips purse into syllables I'm unable to hear. Wanting to imprint my hand on his cheek as compensation for half a year of deception. But that wouldn't satisfy me. It wouldn't give me what I deserve. If he wants to play, I'm game.

I recover from my thoughts to engage Kaleb with my willingness into somatic closeness. I give him what he wants, so I can take exactly what I need from him.

I offer a crooked smile. "Everything *will* change after this… Don't say I didn't warn you."

He nods. "I'm ready."

Chapter 9

The Assessment

I vowed to never be anything other than friends with Kaleb, but he brought this on himself. All the men in my life have stolen something from me through manipulation and self-serving intentions. But I am no longer in a giving mood. Kaleb wasn't just a guy, he was a friend. At least I thought anyway. Now, he's, my conquest.

Kaleb awakens fully clothed, stretching and cooing like a joyful infant. I roll over in the opposite direction, nervously pretending to be asleep, hoping he will leave immediately. I feel his weight shift from the bed, followed by intermittent tiptoeing down the hardwood hallway. Moments later, I hear the doorknob twist and close. A weight lifts. I release a sigh of relief. The last thing I want is to have an unnecessary conversation about how things shouldn't be awkward.

Staring at the phone on my nightstand, I debate calling Blithe. *Am I ready to hear her wrath from my night of what she would call, bad decision-making? Am I ready to face her motherly scalding?* I walk over to the bay window in my bedroom. *Maybe God can tell me what to do.* Slowly scrolling through my contacts, I take a deep breath and make the call.

Sharing the details of my intimate bedroom decorum with Blithe has never been unnerving until today. She is in shock and awe after disclosing the wild rides I've been on in the last 36 hours.

Blithe chokes. "THREE MEN IN TWO DAYS!"

"I know it's more than usual, but I'm an adult and have it under control."

"I don't think you do. Franchesca, I love you, but this is a problem and will turn into a catastrophe if you allow it." Blithe clears her throat to compose herself. "Where is this coming from?"

This question urges my eyes to glaze over. She knows me. I've been scouting for talent for a long enough, that this question seems irrelevant. Recently, I may have added a few more players to the team, but it's no different.

"I don't know what you're talking about."

"When's the last time you spoke with Jamaal."

"When I saw him with Little Miss Floral dress." I releasee a sigh of frustration. "What does he have to do with anything?"

"Everything." A moment of silence accompanies the call. "Before, you were only fulfilling your carnal needs. It didn't matter if you engaged in it because it wasn't an overwhelming desire. It was more entertainment. *Then,* you met a guy who made you feel important. A guy who catered to all your desires, even the ones you didn't know you had. Even though you didn't want anything remotely smelling like a committed relationship, emotionally, you were already in one. You became attached to him. So, when you saw him with someone else, you felt a loss and experienced what that loss felt like over time. Now, you're trying to compensate for it with these men. These men make you feel wanted, but after the physical is over, you still crave the other parts of your relationship with Jamaal. Since you have yourself convinced that you don't want that part, you just look for more sex to feel a connection."

"What am I supposed to do with that, now?" I blurt in confusion.

"Call Jamaal and find out what really happened. You only know what the situation looked like from your perspective."

"He made his choice. He hasn't called, sent a text, or written a letter. Jamaal can stay right where he is."

"You said he apologized and sent flowers. Does that mean nothing?"

My irritation with Blithe turns to impatience. I am not in the state of mind to positively receive her caring diagnosis. The need to escape this conversation overwhelms me. A mental eruption is at its precipice.

"STOP!" I pause for a moment for a deep breath. "Blithe, just stop. Jamaal is gone, and so are Xander and Kaleb. What I once had with them is diminished, and I have and will continue to deal with it in my own way."

We listen to the absence of sound on both ends of the receiver.

"Fine. Figure it out on your own. I hope you don't ruin yourself in the process. But I love you."

Blithe ends the call without allowing me another response. *Maybe she's right. The woman does have a Ph.D. Maybe I should see what Jamaal's side of the story is. But what good would that do?*

I flop backward onto my bed, phone still in hand, starring into it as if it's going to provide me with answers. My life is fine the way it is without emotional instability. Jamaal and all the rest have only loomed over the decadence a relationship should provide. The more I think about the whirlwind my past has created, the more I need an outlet. Jamaal could be just that.

Scrolling through my call thread, his number stares me in the face, and I stare right back, taking a few moments to decide if this is what I want. If this is what I need. I close my eyes to grapple with logic and desperation. Stubbornness and frustration. *What to do? What to do?*

108

Chapter 10

The Reconnection

I'm sopping wet, enjoying a caramel-flavored coffee at my neighborhood brew shop on another rainy day, being comforted by its warmth. Needing a quiet public place to relax after being a prisoner of my thoughts. So much has gone on in my life recently and trying to make sense of it all has become exhausting. Usually, I call Jamal for relief, but I don't know if can do that now. I can't count how many times I've scrolled to his number in my phone, only not to call. That's another prison I'd like to release myself from. Clashing thoughts between wanting to make him feel my frustration or being in his presence for personal gratification.

So, I text Kaleb, instead. Luring him into a weekend with me at a luxury hotel for the weekend. Of course, he excitedly agrees.

Taking another joy-filled sip of coffee, I hear someone speak my name. Opening my eyes, I see the last person I ever want to see. The person I've wanted to avoid forever. The man who destroyed me. The one who turned me into a preying mantis… Xander. *I'm much too unstable for this.*

Releasing a sigh of irritation. "What are you doing here?" I asked.

"You've been avoiding me, so this seemed like the only way I could talk to you."

"So, you've been stalking me?"

"You're just as beautiful as I remember. I always loved you with wet hair." He reaches for my hair.

I quickly retreat from his touch, sitting silently in disbelief. I can't manifest enough energy to respond to this foolishness, so I patiently wait for the purpose of this conversation to unfold.

"Frachesca, I've been wanting to tell you some things I thought you should know."

"And?"

"I'm sorry for everything. I did want to marry you, and I still do, but I was still in love with my ex-girlfriend. When you saw me having dinner with her, I was trying to figure out if I still had feelings for her. I needed to find that out before I could move forward with you, and I did that. There wasn't the love I thought there might be with her, but you were so angry, you left me no time to ever share that with you."

"Well, that's fantastic. I'm glad you figured that out two years later. But did you forget how many times you lied to me about meeting with her? How you never told her we were engaged? Who knows if you two slept together while trying to figure out your damn feelings, but you'd never tell that part. I only know you as a liar, a manipulator and a coward. If you truly wanted to be with me, you would be. I'm almost certain you spent the last two years with her. So, what do you want other than trying to clear your self-absorbed conscience? Get it all out now, so I don't have to see you again."

"I realized the reason why I proposed to you. Why I want you to be my only one. I want us to rekindle what we had."

I laugh hysterically and choke on my sip of coffee. "This conversation is unnecessary. I already know you're a terrible person."

"I see you still have your wit." He responds dryly.

"And I see you're still standing here."

"I know you're still upset with me, and I'm prepared for that, but I know we can work through it."

"You were simply a bad choice. I own that mistake, but I refuse to repeat it."

"Please Franchesca, just think it over. Think of all the times we shared. They weren't all bad, not even most of them."

I grow tired of his pleading, so I put all my energy into sipping my coffee until it's compelling enough for him to leave.

"Mmm, they have great coffee here. You should get a cup." Turning my back to him.

Why would Xander think he could weasel his way back into my life with that sad excuse for an apology, especially after two years of nothing? He thought the grass was greener on the other side, and it died, so now he's trying to come back to my well-manicured lawn. I could beat him with a garden hoe for being so selfish.

Several minutes pass as his lips continue to move, spewing words that I refuse to hear. My continued silence seems to awaken his senses that I haven't been listening and he removes himself from the table.

Finishing my second cappuccino, I notice the rain has stopped, so I pay for my morning addiction and decide to indulge myself in a walk. The sun begins to peak as I pass my building and head to the park. My mind is clear. No incessant thoughts of how complicated my life has gotten. Even the deafening sounds of traffic became background noise. I refuse to allow the expectations of others to control how I move or what I do. I'm taking my life back.

My lips finally purse together to awaken my face for the first time in two weeks. My mind is racing like airplane tires on the tarmac when I realize I've walked six miles and there was no way I'm going to walk back. I hail a cab, and it begins to rain again.

Removing the keys from my handbag, I see Xander approaching me from the elevator, holding a bouquet of my favorite flowers. *What is happening right now?*

Wearing a large grin, he says, "These are for you!"

Rolling my eyes, I put the key in the door. "Yeah, I assumed since you're at my doorstep with them."

"I remembered they were your favorite."

"Yup, they're still my favorite. Why are you here?"

"I just wanted to give you a reminder that I can be gracious." He chuckles.

"So, your plan is to try to win me back with flowers? I really hope you kept the receipt. Excuse me, I'd like to go inside."

I step in front of the door.

"Am I keeping you from something… or someone?" He quickly blurts, while stepping in my path.

This guy really has some nerve. He doesn't know the Franchesca I am today. If he keeps this up, he's going to get to know her first-hand, but not in a good way.

"YES! You're keeping me from getting ready for work. I only have a few hours."

"A few hours? Can I come in to talk because you aren't being very receptive to my sincere advances."

"NO! You've done enough talking for the day. Thank you."

I quickly shove him to the side, unlock the door and slam it in his face. Xander is the type of guy who's persistent when he wants something and won't give up until he gets it. He's expecting me to forgive him instantly because apologies and flowers are magic band-aids. This is how it always was. I couldn't have the necessary time I needed to heal because it didn't benefit him. He wanted instant gratification, and from the looks of it, things haven't changed. I'm not sure what his next attempt will be, but I'm not interested.

***

It's been about a month since I've seen Xander. Thank heavens because I don't know how long I could stomach being semi-cordial. Plus, work has been ridiculously busy with the end-of-the-year reports due. My mind has been all numbers and blueprints. That is until all the talk about Valentine's Day, and I remember I haven't had a real Valentine in four years. Actually, three years. I'll just end up doing what I always do. Take myself out for some fine dining and seek out a single guy to fill the rest of the evening. On second thought, I could call Kaleb, but it's Valentine's Day and I don't want to give him any ideas. I might just go home after dinner and drink wine until I no longer can fight slumber.

A knock at my office door interrupts…

"Come in."

"Franchesca, you have a delivery, but there's nothing on the manifest this week. Should I let him up?" My assistant asks.

"Who is it from?"

"Boston City Florist."

Who would be sending me flowers? Jamaal?

"Send it up."

Several moments later, my assistant brings the delivery to my office. It's a lavish bouquet of white lilies and purple tulips in a rose gold vase. They're beautiful! I try to imagine who they could be from and think of Kaleb. He sends me gifts even though I ask him not to.

There's a card hanging from the stem, and I began to read it:

To my beloved, I want to bring a smile to your face as you bring one to mine!
- Xander

Tilting my head backward in mental exhaustion. *Was I not clear?* Last time I checked, no means I'm not interested. Which also means no more flowers. *How does he know where I work?* I press the call button on my office phone for my assistant.

"Julia! Would you come to my office, please?"

She opens the door again.

"Would you mind disposing of these?"

"But they're so pretty."

"Well, by all means, enjoy them." I smile.

Her face lights up as she removes the vase from my office to place them on her desk. After a long melodramatic day at the office, I finally lock up. As I turn to leave, I'm reminded of Xander when I see the flowers on Julia's desk. At least they have a good home.

Somehow, this year's Valentine's Day became less of an afterthought and more prominent in my mind. Maybe, it was the feeling of being wanted by someone special after receiving flowers. That

114

someone I've been thinking of was Jamaal. *How does a kind gesture from one man make me think of another?* More importantly, why am I thinking of him at all when Valentine's Day is meant for love, and all we had was lust?

Walking to my car, I am quickly reminded of how frigid the weather is, leading me to postpone my grocery stop. Suddenly, Chinese food delivery sounds a lot more convenient.

I dig through my large handbag to retrieve my cell, scroll the call log and press the number. A deep raspy voice answers.

"Hey Kaleb, Happy Valentine's Day!"

"Oh, wow! How lucky am I to get a call from you today. I was meaning to call you."

"I'm sure you were busy, as you've been lately. Why don't you stop by for some Chinese?"

"It's freezing!"

I exhale in frustration, wanting to break the cycle of my Valentine's Day tradition. Afterall, today is for me, not for him.

"I'm sure I can think of some creative ways to warm you up when you get here."

"That sounds like a plan. I'm glad I waited around for you."

I'm sure you are.

I press 'end' on the call screen without saying good-bye.

I beat the traffic on the way home, which is a highlight of my day because there have been ridiculous accidents all week due to the freezing rain.

Finally, home sweet home. All I want to do is shower, get into my sweats, feed my face and try to forget about Jamaal. I still haven't made that phone call, and it's been plaguing me. I've stared at his name in my cell. I've pressed send and immediately ended the call before it started to ring. Maybe one of these days, my courage will outweigh my pride. A part of me wonders if he's identifying with me in this way, and that's why he hasn't called either. He should man up and call so I don't have to. *What would I say? I secretly want you to suffer, but I miss you?*

The knock at the door startles me from the comfort of my sofa. I twist the door open knowing who holds the space on the other side. I softly take his hand to guide him inside and close the door behind him.

"Nice of you to make it over so quickly." I entice.

"Well, you made it sound worth the travel."

He follows me to the bedroom and I aggressively push him to the bed and I begin to peel off my

115

outer layers, as he watches. Kaleb lifts his arm toward me to seemingly touch my bare skin, but I slap it and remain feet away..

"I think I like where this is going," he grins.

I acknowledge him with a smile as I close my eyes to envision it's Jamaal who's laying in front of me. I caress my own skin to prepare myself for what's to follow. With Jamaal I don't have to. I'm going to give Kalab more than one reason to want *all* of me in every way. He has no idea what he's started and should've been more careful.

***

It's hump day, and I've worked so hard that I'm now only ankle-deep in business reporting, so I decide to take an early lunch. I might even take Julie; hell, I'm feeling generous. I reach for the intercom to ring Julie, but she buzzes me first.

"Franchesca, Blithe is here to see you."

"Okay, great! Send her up."

What a surprise! Blithe never visits me at work unannounced. Maybe I'll take a raincheck on lunch with Julie. I need a girl chat. Especially after the last time we spoke. It didn't end on the nicest terms. I refresh my makeup for the love of my life, since that's clearly who she had become. The door opens. I stare in the mirror, but the reflection behind me isn't Blithe.

"WHAT ARE YOU DOING HERE? The audacity of you pretending to be Blithe so I'd send your sorry ass up here!" Making a b-line for the intercom on my desk to call for security.

"Don't be upset, love. If I said it was me, you wouldn't have let me up."

"Well, that should tell you something, shouldn't it?" Listen Xander, I've tried being nice and patient in your several attempts to show up where you aren't wanted, but I'm over it and over you. I can appreciate you wanting to rekindle what we once had, but it's not worth it to me."

"I see you got the flowers I sent you."

"What is wrong with you? Did you suffer a head injury recently, and the result is short-term memory loss? Clearly, a sane person would have gotten the hint already."

"I hear you, and I know you're upset with me, but you're not understanding how much I love you. You don't understand how much I want a second chance to show you I'm the one for you."

I double blink in amazement at the forcible affection being shoved into my life. I'm not sure how many ways I have to say I'm not interested.

I smile seductively. "Well… You *can* show me one thing."

His eyes widen. "See, I knew you'd come around."

"The back of your head as you walk out of my damn door!"

"Franchesca, you aren't willing to give me one last chance? It's such a small request. Just let me take you out for Valentine's Day. You need to eat, right? Why not let me pay for it?"

I sigh at his desperate attempt for a reconnection. Thinking about his request, I'd rather have dinner alone, but maybe if I go, he won't keep showing me his ridiculous face. Then I could say I tried.

"I'll think about it, and until you hear from me, I don't want to see you popping up. Do you understand what I'm saying to you?"

"Yes! Yes!"

"You can leave now. I'm going to lunch, and NO, you can't take me, come with me, or follow me." I look him directly in the eyes.

***

It's been almost a week since I've seen or heard from Xander. I still haven't called about the belated Valentine's Day dinner he invited me to. Which is laughable in more than one way. Part of me is hoping Jamaal would call, or I'd conjure up some spirit to force me to call, but I still haven't gotten there yet. *What do I want from him? Love? Companionship? Sex?* I have yet to figure that out, either. I don't remember what it feels like to jump in with both feet and have blind faith, but maybe it's time. *Or I could just rip my heart out right now.* Getting into a monogamous relationship is unspoken permission to be destroyed. As for Xander, I could go to dinner with him. It's food and it beats staying home. *Am I really saying this?* I lazily pick up the phone and call Xander to confirm the invitation.

It's the big belated V-Day dinner has promised, and Xander has done all the chivalrous things a woman would expect when being courted. The opening of doors, pulling out my chair, standing if I left the table and pouring my wine first. So far, things have been coasting and haven't turned into a regrettable decision.

"What happened to your ex- girlfriend? Did you leave her too?"

He chuckles. "At first it was great, but things changed, and I realized what I wanted in a woman I already had in you."

I stare at him coldly as he smiles, thinking that his response is endearing, but I won't be fooled.

"It's funny how things work out that way."

"Chesca, I know I hurt you and I'm just looking for you to open up just enough to see that I can repair what I've done, so we can be happy together."

"I'm happy. I do what I want, to whom I please. What else is there?"

"What else is there? There's being effortlessly happy and in love with another person who cherishes you."

Hunching my shoulders at the idea of being in love again. I was effortlessly in love with Xander, and he stole my desire to let anyone else get close enough for me to fall for. In addition to Kaleb's manipulation, and the heart throbbing confusion associated with Jamaal, the odds aren't getting better.

"Just give it some time, Franchesca and you'll learn to forgive and love me forever."

I laugh at his pursuit of dominance. He wants me so bad he can taste it. Seemingly willing to do and say anything to make it happen. Maybe, even allowing himself to be tortured through this process. Besides, how would I know if he's being genuine? It seems he goes through cycles of wanting what he can't have, then throwing it away once he has it. Afterall, Xander is the best liar I know. He only looks out for himself. What he wants, he gets, considering he grew up with a silver spoon attached to his upper lip. It's time for me to devise a little plan of my own. I'll give him what he wants, but much more of what he doesn't.

119

Chapter 11
The Call

It's been two weeks since the initial struggle began of making the decision to call or not to call Jamaal. I'm not sure what I want from him. Part of me just wants to return to the way things were between us. Rediscover the passion and excitement. The other part wants to let him go, but I can't seem to release the his mental grasp he has on me. Maybe Blithe was right. Jamaal is a loss, and I need closure to get him out of my life. Picking up my cell, I dial the number and it starts to ring. I pace the room, convincing myself not to disconnect again. Then I hear his voice.

"Hi," he breathlessly whispers.

I hesitate… The sound of his voice cuts through me like a knife. Smooth and without resistance. Hearing the relief in his voice. Feeling the juxtaposition of love and loss.

"Hello?" he greets again.

"Hey." I match his tone.

"Hey," he sounds relieved. "I've been meaning to call you, Franchesca, but I didn't think you'd want to talk to me."

"I would've answered. I assumed you moved on, so I did the same."

Jamaal's voice saddens. "Oh… Franchesca, Lyza and I aren't anything. My buddy was trying to get my mind off you, but I couldn't."

"Oh, she has a name. That's great." I condescend. "Are you still seeing her?"

"I've been too focused on finding a way to win you back."

A short lull presents itself in the conversation. I have no idea what to say. He's been trying to get back in my good graces, and I've been focused on how to push him away.

"I'm sorry I called. I should go." Rushing to end the call.

"Franchesca, WAIT! I want to see you."

Spending time with Jamaal usually means one thing, and I am up for the task, but a piece of me just wants to stare into his beautiful eyes.

I gleefully accept the invitation. "You can stop by in a couple of hours."

Obviously, we both have some growing up to do, but now I take comfort in knowing we're on the same page. He had been wanting to hear from me, and I from him. Fear and rejection stopped us from going after what we wanted. If I hadn't swallowed my pride to make that call, would we have reconnected? Had I not needed closure, would I have called? Would Jamaal still be swimming in thoughts of possible rejection? Sometimes stepping out on a limb can be worth it if the result is getting what you were hoping for all along.

I toss my phone on the bed and bounce around the room with elation. There's a weight of 2-tons lifted off my shoulders. Feelings begin to resurface, and feeling like I haven't in a long time. The excitement of spontaneity to come, the passion that will soon fill my soul and the warm presence of Jamaal's tenderness wrapped around me. I calm myself, so I can plan how the evening will unravel. My mind races with every possible outcome, and before I know it, an hour has passed. Carefully choosing my blue and white rhinestone bustier lingerie set, I catch a glimpse of myself in the mirror. It is stunning! I wonder what Jamaal's reaction to this work of art I've layered myself with will be.

Allowing myself to break away, I light my favorite scented candles positioned around the condo. Jamaal will be here any minute, so I remove the Sauvignon Blanc from the fridge. Pouring two glasses, but I consume them both. My anxiousness appears to settle. As I refill the glasses, the doorbell sounds. I sashay over and twist the knob.

He drops his bag of groceries. "FRANCHESCA!"

I smirk. Not exactly the reaction I was thinking of, but it's entertaining, just the same. Placing my full glass on the coffee table, I help with the spilled groceries.

"I'm sorry. It wasn't my intention to startle you."

We both laugh as we pick up the spilled groceries and place them on the countertop. I see his eyes shuffle, mirroring all of my movements.

"What's all this?"

"I thought I would make us lunch or early dinner… or linner... or dunch."

"Okay, I got it… Food." I smile.

Jamaal laughs nervously, and I notice his eye contact with me is becoming very minimal.

"Is everything okay, Jamaal?"

"Yeah, everything is great!" he shouts.

My eyes instantly widen at the sudden increase in volume, and I blankly stare upon his face. This man is yelling at me, and I'm standing two feet away.

"It's that your inside voice is on 100, and I think we should take it down to about 10. Is it the lingerie that's making you nervous?"

"I'm excited to be here with you, but it is *very* difficult to look at you while you're wearing that."

Raising one eyebrow as I fold my arms. "Excuse me."

"You look amazing. Trust me, I rather have my hands on you than fiddling with this onion." He tosses the onion back and forth in his hands.

"So, what's the problem?"

Clearing his throat. "I, um… can't engage in sexual activities for two months." Shifting his eyes from left to right.

Trying not to panic. "What? Why?! What's wrong with you?"

"Nothing!" Jamaal defensively blurts. "I'm participating in a study for male enhancement, and sex would skew the results." Lowering his eyes.

If he's having difficulties with his manhood, this isn't going to work for me. What else could there possibly be between us?

"Why would you do that? Do you need money?"

"Franchesca… no! I'm supporting a friend."

"What kind of friends do you have? None of this makes any sense?"

"Can we *please* change the subject? And your outfit! I'm struggling, trying *not* to focus on you and trying not to chop off my thumb.

I honestly can't argue with that. I could, but what would be the purpose? I wouldn't get what I thought he came over for. I thought the expectations of this visit were etched in stone from our previous encounters. Why would he not disclose that his equipment is out of service, but instead show up with a bag of groceries? There was no discussion of food preparation.

 I walk to the bedroom to change into something more unappealing, sweatpants and a T-shirt. I slide back into the kitchen in my socks, take a bow, and happily question…

"Is this better for you, or should I throw some rollers in my hair to finish the look?"

He laughs. "It doesn't matter, you'll always be gorgeous, but for the next two months I can only handle the least amount of sexy you have."

He leans over the counter, kisses me on the lips, and continues sautéing the onions in the sizzling skillet. In the lull of conversation, I sip my glass of wine and realize I feel wanted. I feel happy. Jamaal makes me feel like an impeccable treasure. Not only with his words, but also his actions. All this time he knew the only thing I wanted was the physical and he gave that to me with no pressure. He's also made me feel and experience things I often try to deny. I feel like a woman when I'm with him; I feel cherished and safe. This isn't what I signed up for. Our relationship will be absent of sex for two months. How will that work, considering that's what Jamaal and I are built on? Oddly enough, I don't think I'm willing to walk away because of it. However, the thought does cross my mind.

Am I going to be afraid of feeling an emotional connection for the rest of my life?

Maybe. I only know how I feel in this moment. There are no promises. Tomorrow's emotional baggage could be a lot heavier, and in fight or flight, I'd choose the latter.

Chapter 12
The Tables Turn

After dinner last night with Jamaal, I want to see him again. I want him to remember why he's in my life and I don't want to forget how great we are together. He's given me more than any other, but the next three months will be difficult for me. The idea of waiting around for him to be able to fulfill my needs seems unnecessary. *I wonder if he's expecting me to wait?*

The doorbell sounds. *Maybe it's Jamaal coming to rethink our arrangement.* Without checking the peephole, I swing open the door in my t-shirt, and quickly regret it.

"Hey sunshine! You didn't have to get all dressed up for me."

Immediately aggravation consumes me. "Haven't you heard of a telephone? What do you want this time, Xander?"

"I *want* to surprise you with breakfast. Blueberry muffins and hazelnut coffee. Your favorite!" He offers me the recyclable coffee cup.

I take a sip. "You can't just keep popping up. It's becoming exhausting repeating myself."

"Well, I don't consider dropping by my girlfriends house to surprise her with her favorite indulgences a problem."

I clear my throat in an effort not to choke. "Excuse me? Girlfriend? I'm not anyone's girlfriend, especially not yours."

Both his eyebrows lower. "You said you would give me a chance when we had dinner."

"That meant I would give you an opportunity to show you aren't the low-down scum case I know you to be. We are not together, nor am I committed to you. Prove yourself first, and I'll think about making a decision."

"I've been proving myself. I've been sweet, buying you flowers and pouring my heart out to you."

"Those are all nice things, Xander, but I can't trust you. You're a habitual liar and from my point of view, the only reason you're here is because your last relationship didn't work out how you thought. So, excuse me, if I don't jump on the Xander-wagon because you bought me flowers and paid for a coffee."

"Franchesca, I am trying, but it's impossible if you don't try with me. You keep holding on to the resentment you have for me instead of letting me in."

I pause at the seemingly sensical statement.

"You're right." I enjoy another sip of coffee. "I'll ponder that. Thank you for the muffins and coffee. You can let yourself out."

He's the last person I'd take relationship advice from, but he's right. I'll never get him off my back if I don't at least try to pretend I enjoy being in the same room with him. Seeing his face again

126

reminds me of our past, and I've tried to forget as much of it as possible. Past thoughts travel through my mind, and I can't bear to make myself vulnerable again. He's done some despicable things just to hurt me, and even though there would be an occasional apology, there would always be another painful deed. He left an invisible brand on me, rendering me incapable of any sentiment of intimacy or trust.

Why would he come back to me after all these years? He could easily find someone new. Why me, after all that he's done? *Is it for personal redemption or a last chance at true love?* I loved that man with everything I had, even after discovering all his flaws. But, he threw me away like last weeks recyclables. I didn't matter. I never did. I was a place holder until he found someone better. I was the person he could manipulate into being what he wanted, until it became inconvenient for him. He is the taker of love and the giver of NOTHING! He doesn't care about being with me. The sooner I relieve my anger toward him, the sooner *this* can be done.

***

It's been about a month since Xander's last visit, and he seems to be taking my advice. He offered me the key to his apartment. I doubt I'll ever use it, but it's a good start for him. He's been in California preparing for a red-carpet event, Innovative Inventions. It'll be taking place here in Boston this evening. He asked me to be his date, and I felt I had a responsibility to say yes.

Consulting the mirror for a final beauty check, the doorbell rang. *Who is it now?* Pressing my face to the tiny hole in the door. To my surprise, Xander is on the other side.

I squint my eyes. "I thought we were meeting at the event?"

"I decided to come back early to be with you, and I have something you'll be wearing for the red carpet. Open it!" He shoves the garment bag into my chest.

I unzip the bag, and out spills a sparkling red train of sequin. This is literally a red-carpet gown. My bottom jaw drops in awe that he would offer such an elaborately thoughtful gift. I have never worn something so elegant. I rush to the bedroom to slide myself into the beautiful fabric. It's detailed with a strapless, sweetheart neckline, a low plunging back, a thigh-high front split and a train that could trip five people walking behind me. Strutting to the living room with my new head-to-toe look, Xander stands waiting.

"HOLY CRAP!" he yells.

Gasping, I begin to look around at the dress. "What's wrong?!"

"Nothing. You look... I don't think I've ever seen you look like this before. My God!" He adjusts his tie.

I'm unsure of how to receive the compliment. "Um, thanks. Are you ready to go?"

Xander walks toward me placing his hands on each of my hips, pulling my body close, chest to chest, then kisses my lips. My muscles tense as my fingers curl into the palm of my hand. I'm trying not to ruin his night, and luckily the moment passes. He looks upon my face as I reveal the guise of a smile to conceal my apprehension. Approaching the door, he interlocks his hand in mine, then suddenly stops and turns to me.

"I want you to know that I never stopped loving you."

I give no response. The only thing I have to offer is an appreciative smirk. It seems as though the simple gesture is sufficient, and we continue toward the door.

We arrive at the Cambridge Masonic Temple, an elegant place to dine and mingle. There are flashing lights from eager media outlets, crowds of indistinct chatter, and excitement consuming the venue. This could be a career-altering event for him. I'm proud that he is achieving the level of success he's always wanted, but entering the building, I have second thoughts about being here. The plethora of red-carpet photos being captured of Xander and I, him transitioning me into multiple poses so they can catch the perfect one, seems superfluous. I feel like I'm part of a dog and pony show.

Finally, walking inside, leaving the reporters behind, I feel a small bit of relief. There are several ostentatious displays of admiration for various inventions. Guests are everywhere. Gliding across the carpet, sitting at round tables or standing at the bar. It reminds me of the Auto Show, except more magnanimous.

Suddenly, a colleague of Xander's approaches for a short conversation. This is when I realize that wearing a fictitious grin is going to weigh me down.

"Hey Xander, glad you could make it! This must be the lovely Colleen?"
I raise my eyebrows, and tilt my head toward Xander. *If looks could kill.*

He chokes on his saliva. "No, no. This is my girlfriend, Franchesca. This is Dillon, the head of engineering at my company."

Extending my hand. "I'm not his girlfriend, but It was very nice to meet you Dillon. Excuse me while I leave you gentlemen for a more sparkling flavor of company."

Making B-line toward the bar, I try to conceal my anger, but it is becoming more difficult. *Who the hell does Xander think he is introducing me as his girlfriend?* Just because I decided to give a bit of leeway and attend this pretentious function, does NOT mean we are a couple. I thought I made that clear, but it seems that someone's lenses are a bit foggy. All this pretending is going to give me an ulcer. *And who is Colleen?*

"BARTENDER!" I snap. "I need a Sauvignon Cabernet, please."

While waiting for my beverage, I decide to take a moment to calm myself before I behave out of character. If I'm going to go through with this plan, I need to learn to control my emotions. The bartender places my glass on a napkin and nods his head.

"Thanks." I offer apologetically for snapping.

Wrapping my freshly manicured fingers tightly around the base of the glass, wanting to throw it across the room at Xander, but I opt to finish it in a few gulps.

"Excuse me, bartender. May I have another?"

Knowing I have a second glass of wine on its way, I relax and enjoy a bit of people-watching. Their body language as they glide across the room, the pleasant façade, and the need for acceptance is quite entertaining. I've never been one to try to become someone I'm not, to appease the masses. It seems exhausting.

"There you are Franchesca!"

"Yup. You found me." I express dryly. "I'm wearing a red sequin dress. It couldn't have been more difficult."

"Are you having a good time?"

"Well, I'm sure with more cocktails and a proper meal, my boredom has the potential to subside."

"So, you're not having a good time?"

"Xander, we haven't been here long enough to even start having a good time. All I need you to do is keep a glass in my hand and hors d'oeuvres on my plate. I'll be fine."

"I've always loved your sense of humor." He kisses me for the second time.

We stand at the bar in silence, people watching through two different lenses. My lens is for entertainment. I consider browsing the inventions, until a blonde woman catches my attention. She's wearing a floor-length gown, carrying the train in one hand and her wine glass in the other. Her feet quickly pass one after the other. With the distance closing, nervousness sets in. She approaches Xander and me and swiftly splashes her beverage in Xander's face. I lift my arms as the cast off of her drink lands on the front of my dress. I casually shuffle a few feet away to listen to what he has done to this woman while dabbing my dress with napkins.

He pulls his handkerchief from his breast pocket, and pats his face, while reaching out for me. "Franchesca, This is…"

I interrupt. "I don't need an introduction. I know who she is." Holding my palm toward him.

The blonde woman forces her empty glass onto the bar top, and the pieces shatter. Ignoring the mess, she raises her voice for all to hear.

"You untrustworthy, conniving, miserable excuse for a man. You think you can toss me away like I never existed? No note, no call, and no reason? You said you were going on business trip. I haven't heard from you in 2 months. Then you stop answering my calls. YOU SELFISH COWARD! As long as Xander is happy, nothing and no one else matters. You spend so much time traveling, trying to fulfill your idea of a perfect woman, but you are nowhere near the idea of a perfect man. And did you think I wouldn't notice my $5,000 red sequin gown was missing and that your little girlfriend is wearing it? I WANT IT BACK, NOW!"

She swiftly approaches me, clenching her teeth. With both arms forward, she begins tugging at the zipper at the back of the dress. Xander launches himself over to me, places both hands on her shoulders and pushes her away.

"SECURITY!" he calls while pointing at the blonde woman.

"Franchesca, don't believe anything she says. I purchased that dress for you."

"If that's the truth, we can return the dress tomorrow from the retailer you purchased it from. This dress is too extravagant of a gift for me to accept from you anyway."

He stutters for an answer, but nothing manifests. It's a shame that I'm forced to take the word of a stranger over someone I almost married. He's as charming as a prince in a fairytale, but I've found that most of it is a facade. Xander is an emotional con-artist, and it's about time I take back what he stole.

I slide both hands down the front of the stolen dress to adjust myself, and silently make my way to the exit.

"Franchesca, WAIT!" he yells through the crowd.

I continue to the exit as gracefully as possible, ignoring every word from Xander's lying mouth. But, he will find out soon enough that my love came at a cost that he couldn't pay, and now it's time to collect.

***

Furious, I hail a taxi, and shuffle toward the approaching car while I grab my cell from my clutch.

"Kaleb! Meet me at the Encore Hotel." I snap.

"Well, hello to you too. But it's a bit of late notice, don't you think?"

I take a deep breath, "I'm sorry. It's been a rough night and I'm looking for some company, but I understand if you're busy, I can call someone else."

"No! No. I can meet you. Give me an hour."

"Forty-five minutes." I counter.

"You got it."

I arrive at the hotel, immediately check in, and request a bottle of Kaleb's favorite champagne to be sent to the room. Moët Rosè. I've never tried it, but now is just as good a time as any. Actually, it's the perfect time. I quickly text Kaleb the room number, then tug the small train of my dress along to search for it. *There you are.* I tap the key and enter, heading directly for the high-rise window. The tightness in my chest begins to dissipate as the sights of the city relax me. *I could sure use a—*
There's a knock at the door...

A voice calls, "Room service."

Perfect timing. I scamper to the door and press the lever as it clicks. I've never been so happy to see a stranger. I listen to the squeaks as the bellman rolls the cart to the middle of the room. I gaze in anticipation as the delicious liquid makes contact with the inside of the champagne glass, and soon my palette. He extends his arm to me, glass in hand. I accept the offer, close my eyes, and place the rim on my lips. *Mmm.* I tip the kind man and return to my seat at the window.

"Have a good night, Miss."

I raise my glass in reciprocity.

I lose track of time as I enjoy the beauty of the night but hear a second knock as I glance at my timepiece. *40 minutes.* I grab the bottle sitting in the cart next to me, filling the second empty glass as I approach the door.

"Hi," I push the glass against Kaleb's button-up."

He takes a sip, "Mmm." He moans. "You remembered."

I did." I smirk at him over my shoulder and refill my glass.

Watching him enter further into the room all his wants and needs begin to whirl in my mind.

Every secret desire. Every intimate detail. Every sultry experience he's been wanting to have. Some of them he claims he'd like to wait until marriage so he and his future wife can share them together. *How thoughtful.* As my thoughts spin with delight, a new plan emerges. I will fulfill his every desire tonight, no matter how long it takes. Any little thought he can muster, I will accommodate. His dreams will come true, even those meant for his future. He wanted me *so* bad, and he's had me, but you better believe that now, I've got *him.*

I didn't allow Kaleb to remove my floor length gown as I indulged him as my conquest. He pleads to see my bare skin, but I refuse because tonight is about his vulnerability, not mine. I offer him everything I have. Every move I know and every desire he told. He expresses himself in ways I've never seen from him before. Verbally calling out to me, and even muttered those three unforgettable words. I assume it's from the heat of the pleasure, so I continue to give an exceptional performance.

After he seems to be depleted of all energy, I unravel myself from the bed sheets and fill another glass of delicious bubbly. I savor the taste for one last time.

"You can keep the room for the night." I say between sips.

Kaleb lifts his upper body, "What do you mean? You're not staying the night?"

"I won't be staying with you tonight, or any other night."

His eyes widen, "What are you talking about? I just had the most incredible night of my life with you."

I offer a crooked smile. "How about that? Now you can keep it in your memories because this is done." Finishing the last drop from the glass.

I place my empty flute on the cart as I stride by it on my way to the door. Kalab flings the sheets away from his body to hop from the bed in his bareness. He runs pass me and barricades the door with his body.

Holding both palms toward me. "WAIT! What do you mean this is done?"

I roll my eyes. "Is English not your fist language? You got what you wanted from me Kaleb. You pretended to be my friend, when you were just waiting for an opportunity to sleep with me. You almost begged me to let you experience me, but you're charming so it didn't present itself as desperation."

"I— I… Um… okay. At first. Yes. I would see you every week for months, leaving with a different guy. You're beautiful and kind, so I figured if you're giving yourself to these guys, why not me. But I couldn't just ask if I could take you home. I needed a plan. But now, I like you."

132

I can't believe what I'm hearing. The audacity of this man creating a ruse all in the name of getting laid. Of all the woman available in Boston who are readily available to exist casually with the opposite sex, he thought he needed a plan? *I thought older men were smarter*. But how upset can I be? I'm no better than Kaleb. I stole from him something valuable that he may never get back, while he stole from me something I would've offered him willingly.

I scoff. "Well, guess what, Kaleb? You becoming interested in me was part of my plan that came to fruition tonight. From now on when you think of the best night of your life, who are you going to imagine? ME! Good luck to any other woman who tries to fulfill you, comfort you, or intrigue your passionate sensibilities, because my face will forever be imprinted on the back of your eyelids every time you have a desire."

We continue to stand facing each other, staring blankly into each others eyes as if it's a contest of who will look away first. He casually moves to the side to let me exit the room. I rest my hand on the lever before applying any pressure and lower my head as I replay the previous moment.

"Franchesca?"

I slowly peek over my shoulder.

"Did I never mean anything to you?"

"You did. When I believed you were *actually* my friend."

134

Chapter 13
Reconciliation

During the weeks of evading Xander's every attempt to reconcile, and breaking things off with Kaleb, I have plenty of time to think. Thoughts whirl through my mind like a category five hurricane revisiting all the schemes I had been a victim of. All the lies, embedded in half-truths. All the women that Xander assured me would never become a threat. As I dwell on these moments, I feel as if one thousand blades are piercing my heart again. My eyes fill with liquid anger. Realizing I had given him so much in exchange for so little. Many nights in my past, I cried myself to sleep, hoping for healing that seemed to never come. Hoping for Xander to offer a meaningful apology. But it never came.

I remember it so clearly. Five years ago. The night I followed Xander to what he explained would be a guys' night out, was the beginning of when I became emotionally barren. As I watched him sit across from his former girlfriend, I could only see how he coupled her hand in his, lowered his body to one knee, and gleefully asked her permission to be his fiancé. Witnessing invisible words of affection travel from his lips to hers, my heart plummeted. It receded into an area in my chest where it could never be uncovered again. Surrounded by resentment and anger.

I decided to create my own healing that night. It took five years to master it, but I found my way. I've treated all of them like they've treated me. Disposable. And now they're all just a notch on my designer belt, and Xander will be the biggest one.

My eyes shift toward the sound of Xander's ringtone, and I begrudgingly follow it.

"What?" I say dryly.

"Franchesca, please don't hang up," he pleads.

Quickly reminding myself why I decided to answer. I say, "I've been thinking… You're the only man I've ever fallen in love with. The only one I was willing to vow the rest of my life to. I owe it to myself to offer you a real chance to show me that you're a better man."

"R-really?"

"Since today is my birthday, I'll let you prove it to me. Meet me at Martini Life for lunch and I'll tell you what I want."

I immediately end the call, and a weight seems to lift. Not all. But some. I feel like I will finally have my happy ending. Not the one I hoped for five years ago, but a revised version that just might cure my soul.

***

Xander wastes no time arriving and waves me over to the table he has selected.

"Franchesca, I came back to Boston for you. You can choose to believe Phoenix if you want, but seeing isn't believing. I've had a few slip-ups, but you aren't perfect either. I shouldn't be going through the wringer, but I am. I *said* you are the one I want, right?"

Listening to the wretched words escape his lips, kindles a fire in my chest. He says them as if I should be on his time for how long he should be held accountable for his actions. On his time for how long I'm allowed to hurt or be angry. As if the mere mention of his adoration for me should beckon my immediate loyalty. It's time to redeem myself as a person and as a woman.

"Okay, Xander, I believe you. I'm going to allow myself to give you the one and only second chance you're going to get from me."

"To celebrate, how about I take you out to dinner tonight around six?" he asks.

"I already have dinner plans, but maybe tomorrow."

"Perfect!" He smiles.

He leans over the table, kisses my lips, and leaves me with my margarita. Thoughts of my dinner plans whirl, and a hard-to-swallow lump appears in my throat.

***

Arriving home, I prepare my place for the dinner to take place soon. Pulling down the choice wines and glasses to pair with the surprise assortment of food to be prepared. Sifting through my phone for music to set the tone, I run across what was intended to be my wedding song. I usually skip over it in my playlist queue, but I think I'll let it run for motivation. Laying on the carpeted floor of my bedroom, meditating on the lyrics, I hear a couple knocks at the door.

"Hey Jamaal!" I direct him to the kitchen with a smile as he rests two recycled brown bags of groceries on the counter. "How much food do you think we need for two people?" I gasp.

"Well, I'm preparing a tasting menu of all the foods you've wanted to try." He smiles, pulling each element from the brown bags.

My eyes light up at the pure thoughtfulness he's presenting to me. I don't deserve this. His efforts, nor his energy.

"Do you remember our first night together when you were reluctant about any future for us?" Continuing to prep the food. "We've come a long way." He chuckles.

"I guess." Raising my shoulders. "Since abstinence has been forced on me due to your participation in this little experiment. But, you aren't a bad guy to spend time with." I smirk.

I lower my eyes to the countertop, staring at a crumb from this morning. "Maybe we should take a step back for a while. There's some stuff I have to figure out, and I don't want to neglect you in the process."

"What? What stuff?"

"Personal stuff." I spew like an erupting volcano. "I'll share it with you when I can, but I just want to let you know I won't be as accessible."

"You won't get rid of me *that* easily." He returns to the pan of sautéing garlic. Not wanting to ruin the evening, I allow him to have the last word, while shifting my attention to the aroma of the amuse-bouche.

***

I awaken with thoughts of all the delicious food I have left over from last night's dinner. As I walk to the kitchen to reheat the lobster macaroni and cheese, my thoughts shift to the meal I am to share with Xander this evening. I'm not sure how this new beginning of ours is going traverse, but I'm sure my devotion will give me what I'm looking for this time.

After my Saturday cleaning ritual, I begin to ready myself for Xander's arrival. I didn't want to dress too upscale, even-though Xander has a flare for the finer things. We're going to one of several of Xander's favorite restaurants and events. He plans to show me how much he cares for me this month by fine dining me to death. I guess his mentality is, if you throw enough money at it, you'll get what you want eventually. I appreciate his efforts, but time will tell if they are genuine or superficial. I know which one I'm betting on.

We arrive at the establishment, and elements of familiarity waft around me. I've been here before. Jamaal introduced me to an amazing dining experience a few months ago. The tableside flambé, complimentary short-rib, and exemplary service! Five-star ratings across every column if you ask me. So, naturally I'm excited for the evening.

"So, what do you think? Have you been here before?"

I choose dishonesty due to his fragile ego. "No, I haven't. It's glamorous!"

The last time he invited me to an event and discovered I had experienced it previously, he uninvited me.

The maître d' leads us to our table, guides me into my chair and our server appears almost immediately afterward. Xander clears his throat, while giving his tie a wiggle from left to right.

"We want to order a bottle of Perrier Jouet champagne and chocolate-covered strawberries." The server offers a single nod before he retreats to the kitchen.

"When did you become so fancy?"

"I've learned a lot during these years without you. Preparing myself for when I saw you again." He smiles.

My lips begrudgingly purse together with delight at the compliment.

Lowering my head. "I don't know what to say."

We sit staring at each other in silence. My eyes circle the room awkwardly, waiting for the server to return, as Xander continues to flaunt his pearly whites.

"Oh. Thank goodness," I whisper.

The server places the decadent fruit and ice bucket at the center of the table, then gently fills our glasses with carbonated bubbles.

"Anything else, sir?" the server inquires.

"That's it for now. Thanks."

This is the first time alone with Xander when I don't want to kill him. So, all I can manage is to sit in silence, while shoving strawberries in my mouth. *Delicious Belgian chocolate strawberries!* Trying to think of a genuine conversation to have with this man is mentally painful. The only thing I continue to think of is all the hurt as I look him in the face. One minute I remember how good we used to be, then the next, I want to chop him in the throat. But I'm trying. The past is hard to let go of when Xander hasn't done anything to make me see the future.

"Are you okay?"

"I'm… I'm trying."

Gently, he says, "I'm sorry. But, I'll prove to you I've changed."

Not knowing how to feel, my eyes begin to gloss over at the words, and I quickly turn away.

"I can't do this. I'm sorry. I- I need to go." Bringing myself to my feet.

Xander explodes from his chair. "Franchesca!"

"Please don't follow me, Xander."

***

I pick up my car from the valet and race through the darkness, struggling to see the road through the glare of my tears. Pulling my cell from my handbag as soon as I arrive home to call Jamaal, but then I pause, staring at the lit screen. *What would I tell him?* That I just returned from a date with my ex-fiancé, and I'm violently confused? He would never talk to me again. The anger and frustration run through me like lava erupting, and I throw my phone across the room before releasing a crowd beckoning scream. Forcefully exhaling, as I walk into the hall to retrieve my hopefully uncracked phone. Then I call Blithe. I need a release. I have to tell her what's been going on or my head will explode. I need help.

"So, are you thinking of giving him another chance?"

I don't know what to tell her. I don't know what to tell myself. Everything was much easier before tonight. I had a plan.

"I have to think it over." I sigh.

"He's been chasing you for months, 'Chesca. It's been like four years, maybe he did change, but you'll never know if you don't jump in with both feet."

"I jumped in once and got obliterated."

"So, *don't* give him a chance." Blithe huffs. "You're either going to find it in your heart to forgive him and see how happy you could be or drop him."

"That's a lot to try to unpack."

"Well, you better do it quickly because you know he's going to be a bug-a-boo!" She laughs.

She always ends the call with a laugh I didn't know I needed. I love her for that! As lighthearted as the moment was, turmoil once again covers me heavily. Thinking about how to reconcile my feelings for Xander isn't something I thought I'd be facing. I chose to forget his existence and that was working for me. Now, I'm being pulled into emotional quicksand and the only helping hand I see is Xander's.

Will I be too stubborn to grab hold of it?

***

It's been a few weeks since I walked out on Xander at the restaurant, and surprisingly he has been a good sport about it. I'm used to his lack of understanding and empathy. So, dating him again with obvious changes in his personality is a pleasant surprise! He's been the guy I fell for back in college, just with more money. We've taken a helicopter ride just so he could hover over the buildings I've designed. He plans elaborate dating excursions that he knows are my first. We recently returned from a weekend in Niagara Falls. It was wonderful! Dinner in the revolving dining room over the falls, watching through ceiling-to-floor windows as the multicolored lights twinkle underneath its cascade. These weeks have felt like we're meeting for the first time. Making the decision to lower my defenses seems to have been a good one, although the back of my mind periodically wonders with Jamaal.

Jamaal and I still spend time together, just not as much as we used to. With the opening of his new restaurant and the no-sex situation, our relationship is still a bit complicated, but he doesn't need to know that. He thinks everything is great between us, and I'd like to keep it that way because I don't know what I'm doing. I've finally taken a single step of maturity by rekindling with "the one that got away," and I'm happy. Then I intermittently remember how Jamaal makes me feel when we're together, and I begin to question it all. Casually dating them both seems like the best option until I can sort out my emotions. But why does it feel wrong? This is why I don't get involved. As far as Kaleb, I'm just trying to stay as far away from him as possible. The last time we were together, his seduction had nuances of desperation, and I don't need that issue right now.

Xander has been out of town on business for almost a month and that has given me more time to enjoy Jamaal. I miss our sultry excursions, but he's showing me the intimacy I didn't realize I had been craving. Cuddling on the sofa while reading the same book together, engaging in intellectual conversations and enjoying picnics by the river. Every moment with him is divine, but the lulls in my mind often sway toward Xander. Emotions for both men get tangled and have become hard to shake like they're part of my DNA. Like my heart is reluctantly bound to both in incredibly different, but fulfilling ways. How did I go from a satisfying life of physical indulgences to becoming emotionally overwhelmed?

In a few days Xander will be making his return to Boston, so I decide to be one with my thoughts to consider my situation. As I pour myself a glass of white wine, there's a knock at the door. Taking a sip of its deliciousness before striding to the door to look through the peephole. I swing open the door, unwrap my arms and leap in his direction.

"You're home early!" My face beams.

"I couldn't wait to see you! I came straight from the airport." He unzips his luggage. "I need to show you something."

Right after he shoves his hand inside the bag, he quickly puts it in his pocket. Then with both hands, he gently embraces my face to lean in for the first kiss of passion we've shared since our reconnection. My muscles begin to relax, my mind is silent, and my body starts to react.

He gazes into my eyes. "I've loved you for a very long time. I never stopped. My life wasn't better without you in it, and I was stupid to think that it would be. I've lived without you once and I don't want to do it again."

With a continuous gaze, he slowly lowers himself to one knee. And presents me with the most beautiful diamond ring.

"Will you make me the happiest man and be my wife?" holding the ring between his index and thumb.

I. Am. Speechless.

Finally, the man I've always wanted has become the man I've always needed! After college, I never thought the day would come when I could consider being engaged again. But here's the day with a ring in my face and I have to decide. He stares, trying to keep his composure as the beads of sweat ripple over the wrinkles in his forehead, patiently awaiting my response. My heart feels like it's trying to fold in on itself, and I stand, returning his gaze.

"YES! I will marry you!" resting my palm over my lips.

Leaping from bended knee. "I CAN'T BELIEVE IT!" Xander slides the ring on my finger.

It's a perfect fit. Immediately we go out to celebrate. As we valet, Xander announces to everyone outside the restaurant that I'm his fiancé. Clapping and celebratory cheers burst around us. I couldn't be happier. It feels good to be wanted by the man you've always wanted. To be treasured and valued. My life is seemingly coming together.

143

Chapter 14
Retribution

After months of wedding planning, cake sampling, and venue hopping, it's still so surreal. I keep ogling my left hand in disbelief, feeling as if I'm an astral projection watching someone else's life, but it's me I'm seeing. My heart flutters with fear and elation as the days skip closer to "I do," just waiting for him to change his mind. Change his mind as if I don't deserve to be loved. As if I'm not the one offering him my life, effort, energy, love, and time. Often my mind filters through our previous engagement, and emotional turmoil begins to fill my heart. Blithe says I can't allow old hurt to interfere with his new character, and I agree. I told him yes to eternity, and I meant it. I guess I have some healing to do.

Xander has been hands-on through all the planning. Traveling all over the city just to make sure we have everything we've ever wanted for our special day, despite having to fly back and forth to California for work. He's been a dream manifesting into my reality. I spent so much time running from the only thing left to be fulfilled by... love. Fearing someone would imprint the treads of their carelessness onto me, leaving my life with the emotional damage. But all of that is over now.

The wedding is only two months away, and I still haven't had that necessary conversation with Jamaal. The guilt washes over me like a plague whenever I think about it. But today is the day. I need to come clean. He deserves that, no matter how much it will hurt both of us. As I rest my hand on the door to the café to meet Jamaal for lunch, I realize I have my engagement ring on. Staring at its beautiful representation, my heart begins to fall out of rhythm. A beat that I am more than familiar with. An inconsistent thud that offers no comfort or security. Swallowing the thickness forming in the back of my throat as I rest my hand on the door handle, I tremble.

A line forms behind me and I listen to the murmurs of the concerned patrons waiting to enter the cafe. *What is she doing? Is she ok?* Hot flashes overwhelm me as I forcefully shove the ring into my pocket. Holding my breath before releasing a mighty exhale, I push the door open. My eyes scan the room for Jamaal, but there is no sign of him, so I take a seat by the window. We love to watch the passersby and share fictitious lifestyle scenarios of who they are. A montage of moments we've shared consumes my thoughts, and I begin to imagine the hurt and disappointment that will be plastered on Jamaal's face when I tell him I've vowed my eternity to someone else before I gave him a fighting chance. My eyes fill with watery anguish. Then, the sound of my phone startles the stream of tears down my face. I quickly glide the back of my hand across my face. I answer.

"Hey Farnchesca. I'm so sorry. There's an emergency at my restaurant, and I have to handle it. Can we reschedule?"

Music to my ears.

"YES! ... I mean, yeah, no problem. Is everything alright?"

"Nothing your man can't fix… Gotta go."

I giggle at the compliment like a coy schoolgirl as I hang up the phone. Moments pass before resting my palm on my forehead with relief and confusion. *What am I doing?* Removing myself from the window seat, placing one foot slowly in front of the other, thoughts of being a married woman whirl uncontrollably. No longer being present in the moment of having a crush. Walking home accompanied by wobbly ankles with each step, I know I can't keep Jamaal in the dark, but I feel like I'm making a mistake.

After a hazy emotional journey and seeing the doorman, I know I've made it home. I elevate to my floor on the longest ride I've ever experienced. Turning the key and forcing myself over the threshold of my condo. Peeling myself out of my clothes, I feel a need for the largest glass of wine I can get my hands on. As I make my way to the kitchen, I hear a knock at the door.

Xander?

Begrudgingly, I turn the knob and pull the door toward me as the hallway air pushes in. My face fills with amazement! My eyes widen, and the shock renders me speechless. But only for a moment.

"Phoenix?" I whisper as she returns a crooked smile. "What are you doing here? How do you know where I live?" Peaking around the corner of the door frame.

"I've been following Xander to find out what he's been up to since he traded us in for a new life." She continues to smirk.

The audacity of this woman coming to my door unannounced. But more importantly, what does she want from me?

"Well, Xander isn't here. He'll be back in Boston in a few days." Slowly closing the door.

She slaps her palm on the door. "I know *exactly* where he is. He's exactly where he needs to be. At home with his daughter and his wife."

My eyelids flutter. "Excuse me? I'm his wife. At least I *will* be."

I lift my left hand.

She aggressively reaches for my hand and holds it inches from her face. I immediately pull away.

"The first time you put your hands on me, I let it slide. This time I won't." I inform.

I witness the heartbreak pouring over her, and I feel pity. The typical jealous ex-girlfriend doing anything to ruin the potential future of the one she can't stand to lose. Any woman who would go through the lengths of stalking with the goal of sabotage, is psycho. She's giving me Katia vibes, but I'm not walking away this time.

"Are we done here, Phoenix?"

Her gaze never releases from the diamond on my hand as she reaches into her purse. Out came a wallet. She sifts through and pulls out a photo, holding it toward me until I decided to take it. Rolling my eyes, I reluctantly wrap my hand around the photo.

"I already knew you two were married. Xander and I were engaged when you conveniently popped up back in college." Slapping the picture back into her hand.

"Engaged? He was never engaged to anyone except me." She scoffs.

"HA! Why would he tell you? We dated for a whole two years before I witnessed him proposing to you with *my* ring." Staring at her left hand. "I see you still have it."

"WE HAVE A DAUGHTER!" Her voice cracks while showing me a picture from her phone library. "The entire time he's been away from you, he's been with us. LOOK AT THEM!"

I scroll past the first photo to the second, then the fifth to the tenth. I scroll until devastation washes over me. Until I've tortured myself with joyous photo after joyous photo, smiling back at me. I choke on my saliva trying to conjure the English language from my throat, but there is only vomit. *Could this be real?* All this time Xander has spent chasing me and he finally wins me back and he has a whole family? I can't believe he didn't slip up once. It's impossible. *Why would he do that?* He called security to keep her away from *me* at his work gala and called *my* name to stay with him, not hers. Was he returning to California to be with his family all this time, but calling it work? I swallow every emotion running through my body and casually return her phone.

"See, he's not going to marry you. My husband can afford 10 of those rings and give them away as bubble gum prizes. You can't have something that was never yours. He's only in Boston until this new company is fully functional, then he will be back in California full-time."

I have no desire to spark a debate with Phoenix about her "happy" home. I only have enough energy to stand idol and end the conversation by closing the door. My day has gone from bad to worse in a matter of minutes and I don't have enough brain capacity to devote to problem-solving. But I know one thing. There will be a wedding. No one is taking this away from me.

***

The big day is tomorrow, and there hasn't been a word from Phoenix, and Xander hasn't mentioned her visit to my doorstep. I assume she didn't tell him about her little adventure. He's been just as excited about me becoming Mrs. Greene as the day he proposed, and that's what I hoped. Everything is going as planned. He and I visit the venue to check on the final touches we discussed with the wedding planner about. It's beautiful. Purple and silver bouquets, pearl strands draping from the ceiling, and a glass dance floor with lilac petals resting underneath. I imagine everyone in their seats gasping at its beauty.

It almost saddens me that the experience will be short-lived.

Seeing everything in its place, Xander and I go our separate ways for the evening for the customary Bachelor/Bachelorette party, except I won't be having one. I haven't exactly been open to building relationships since college, so Blithe will be the only one there. I didn't announce I was getting married to many people simply because I was skeptical, not even my parents. So, sadly the guests will be 97% those who know Xander. He invited everyone from cousins to business partners. The expected guest count will be around 75 people. But it will still be a very special day for me!

***

The big day has arrived! The day I didn't think I wanted. I never thought I'd have the opportunity, but here it is, staring me down like a burglar in an alleyway. But I refuse to let any more be stolen from me. I'm taking back what's mine, including the ring.

After sending a quick text, Blithe and I arrive at the church, and I'm still not ready. Bustling to the reserved room, Blithe holds at least three pounds of my multi-layer gown as I hold up the front. The bodice is filled with silver, shimmering stones that trail down the top layer of the skirt. Glamorous isn't the word! But sweat begins to stream uncontrollably at the thought of having all those eyes peer at me as I walk down the aisle. I've never done something as incredible and fulfilling as I am about to do. Blithe continues to fasten the corset closure in the back of the gown.

"Suck. It. In." Blithe tugs.

"Am I not supposed to breathe today? Is that it? Maybe I shouldn't have had that big breakfast."

Blithe trailblazes through the tightening of each corset string and forces the zipper all the way up. Depleted from this longer-than-preferred ordeal, I allow my body to plummet onto the less-than-comfortable sofa in the room.

Exhaling shallow breaths. "Why are wedding dresses so unreasonably difficult?"

"I guess they make them with the intention of only having to put them on once." Blithe chuckles.

The music cue for my once-in-a-lifetime entrance brings Blithe and I to a pause. She tries to pull me off the sofa with her pregnancy strength, but I relieve her of the duty and scoot myself to my feet. Making my way to the door with seemingly ten pounds of satin and rhinestones, I inhale deeply. The double doors open, and I glide through the threshold. I hear the immense shuffling of everyone rising to their feet. Blithe trails behind me, ensuring my train is perfect. Gliding down the pastel blue runner, passing each row as each guest gleefully points their camera phone in my direction. My dress sways from front to back as if I'm floating across the floor, trying not to stumble. Peeling my gaze away from the eager guests, my eyes lock with Xander's. His face is flush standing beside his groomsmen as he tries to hide his emotions. I match his delightful visage with subtlety as the runway to the altar reduces to only a few steps.

Standing face to face with the man I've always wanted, but somehow I didn't realize how satisfying this would be. As the officiant begins to recite the traditional script of unity and commitment, I break my gaze to glance into the crowd, seeing how expectant they are of a happy ending.

"Xander, you may recite your vows." The officiant encourages.

You are the only one I truly love. I knew you were the one when I met you back in college. I knew if we were meant to be, I would find you again, and here we are, destined to spend the rest of our lives together. Sharing first experiences. Sharing our first child. I can't wait to make you the mother of my children and my wife.

The crowd begins to murmur at his words as if they know something about them is disingenuous. As if they know something I don't.

"Franchesca, you may continue with *your* vows."

I hand off my bouquet to Blithe, who replaces it with a folded piece of paper. I pause in the moment her hand touches mine, staring at this fold of insignificant paper knowing what's written inside will change our lives. But I decide to wing it. Delight fills my soul with what I am about to say. The guests happily wait for my response as I open my lips…

"What about your wife? Did you tell her the same thing when you left me for her?"

He glances nervously at our audience, flashing an awkward smile, followed by an abrupt exhale.

"What about your daughter? Seems like you've forgotten about her and the fact you have a whole family that you conveniently haven't mentioned."

The crowd gasps, almost in unison, as his secrets are revealed.

Beads of sweat begin to form on his brow. "Franchesca, If you can't trust me, I don't know what we are even doing here. And how dare you try to—"

I refuse to hear another word. "YOU'RE RIGHT! I don't trust you. Why would I? You thought you would come back to old reliable when the life you chose was no longer suiting you. You conned me, then threw me away like last week's leftovers. You played me. Not once, but TWICE! But most of this time you've spent trying to *woo* me, I forced myself to want you thinking I was the problem. But then I received an opportunity to beat you at your own game."

A commotion of yelling ensues beyond the closed doors of the ceremony. All of the guests turn in curiosity toward the doors as they are abruptly swung open by the wife of my fiancé. Xander's eyes widen in what seems like terror. He turns toward her and quickly grabs my hand. Immediately untangling my hands from his grip, I gently place them on each side of his face, waiting until he looks me in the eyes, I whisper… "Checkmate."

His eyes begin to drip. I release his face, reel in my dress, and make a B-line for the exit as Blithe follows, offering a wink of solidarity to Pheonix as I pass her in the aisle. Part of me wants to stay just to see what she'll do to him, but the other part wants to celebrate a job well done.

Blithe has no idea what just happened. I never told her. I needed to do this to avenge the years lost because of him and I didn't want to be talked out of it. He owed me. And now, his debt is paid.

***

Xander has called me every day since the event, and it brings me joy to know that he still has things to say to me, and I will never hear them. But that isn't enough. He has to know I'd never hear them. So, on the fourth day, I text him.

You mean nothing to me. You. Are. Nothing. You could tell me you're on your death bed, and I wouldn't hear one word of it. When you call, it's forwarded to my work assistant's desk, and she's instructed to delete every message you leave. I don't receive one ring from you on my personal line.

Whether she sifts through them before she deletes them is her business. So, I hope you haven't been
embarrassing yourself. ⬚

Blithe has been constantly reminded me that I'm evil and that what I did was wrong. She isn't taking my actions very well, saying that it's out of character for me. She's right. It is. But it was the only way to rectify these last five years. Which were also out of character for me. He changed my life, my outlook on relationships, and how I treated men socially. I knew I couldn't be loved again because I knew there was no way I'd ever give that part of myself to anyone. She thinks I ruined his life. His family. But what about my life? My future family? I saw he and I with those things, as husband and wife. Personally, I don't think I ruined anything; He did that perfectly without my help. I may have hacked his ego, but I'm sure he'll pick up the pieces and con someone else with his façade.

But, Blithe does have the gift of persuasion. After many debates, she now has me considering that maybe I could've handled this differently. I unleashed the rage of the skeletons from my past, and it changed the trajectory of Xander's life savagely. His wife will probably leave with half his money, his child will probably lose respect for him as a father, and he might lose some custody and might be disowned by family, friends, and business partners. He definitely lost, but my win was only short-term.

I presented myself as doing the work of karma, but what will karma have for me?

Chapter 15
Redemption

Months have gone by, and I can't seem to rid myself of the carnivorous nature of guilt. Not to mention the additional heaviness coming from Jamaal trying to forcefully step back into our old routine, but I don't know if I can. Incessantly pacing across my wall-to-wall glass window with my third glass of wine of the evening, I try to self-soothe in the seemingly least self-destructive way. Every day, glass after glass, until the buzz beckons me to bed.

I continue to pace, looking at the street below, somehow hoping an epiphany will materialize, but then my phone rings.

I drag my bare feet across the long nap of the rug toward the glow of the screen as it reveals who's calling. *I can't deal with this right now.* I stare at the device until the rings cease. Only for him to call again… and again.

Releasing a deep sigh before answering.

"Jamaal, I can't give you what you want from me. I'm sorry." I quickly remove the phone from my ear to end the call.

"You're sorry?" he yells. "After all the patience I've had these last few months waiting for you to deal with… whatever it was you were occupied with, all I get is, I'm sorry. You wanted me to wait for you, and I DID."

"I never told you to wait for me."

"Franchesca, did you ever consider why I chose not to move on? I had more opportunities than just the one you walked in on."

"Great. So why aren't you blowing up their phones?"

"Because I love *you*, dummy! I want to be with *you*, but you're fighting every move I make."

I pause. I have an opportunity to retort, but for the first time, I have no words. My chest is whirling with the tension of all my emotions, and I can't discern how I should feel in this moment. This is the first time in my life that a romantic partner has expressed their love for me, and I felt the conviction behind it. Being immersed in a pool of someone else's affection for you is overwhelming.

Is it supposed to be?

"Jamaal, I'm broken." I reveal tirelessly.

"I know. But your brokenness is not a deterrent. It's your unwillingness to put in the effort to no longer be broken. As if you're happy being uncared-for and jilted."

"I'm not happy. The funny thing is, I was happier before the idea of vengeance burrowed into my mind, and now that I've executed it. I don't feel better. I feel like I'm buried underneath it."

"Vengeance? Franchesca, what are you talking about?"

"Never mind that. Just know that even you can't refurbish my broken pieces, even with the love we have."

I disconnect the call before he begins to ask questions that I am *clearly* not ready to answer.

***

Blithe has been encouraging me to consider therapy to help me sort through all of my unwanted emotions. She's always been my partner in crime when I've needed her perspective, but she refuses to be there for me in a professional capacity. Never thought there would come a point in my life that I'd require therapy. But, continuing to tell myself, 'I'll be ok'… 'Just move on'… 'Try to forget about it,' doesn't seem to work, and it's beginning to devastate my soul.

After deciding to finally swallow my pride, I make an appointment with Dr. Samuels. Blithe recommended him, so I feel I will be in good company. Coincidentally, he had a cancelation and there's an opening today. *Lucky me.* I can't say my excitement is overwhelming, but something needs to happen. I check in with the receptionist and wait only a few moments before Dr. Samuels beckons me. Apprehensively placing one foot over the other, and I tip-toe into his office.

"Please, take a seat wherever you'd feel most comfortable."
My eyes pan the room for all the options, and the chaise made me smile. I've always wanted one, but could never find one to match my aesthetic. My grandmother has one, which always made me feel fancy, as no one else I know has one…until now. I quickly stumble in its direction as the doctor turns his chair clockwise for a better view.

Exhaling soothingly. "What made you decide to come talk to me today, Franchesca?"

Thoughts tornado through my mind. Flashes of how my life has been after graduation versus this very moment. Choices I've made and people I've pushed away. Emotionally and mentally… Finding glimpses of relief in the bottom of my wine glasses. Relying on a liquid diet, while my stomach pangs for solid nutrition.

 Life isn't good right now.

"Franchesca?" Dr. Samuels gently inquires.

Slowly lifting my eyes to him. "I'm sorry. I guess everything is the reason why I'm here." Lifting my shoulders like a small child.

"Start from the beginning."

The beginning? I have no idea where that is.

"There's a lot, but mainly, my ex came around wanting to start over, but there was *no way* I was going to fall into his strap for a second time. So, I planned to pay him back for all he's done. I only feel like crap about it because my goodie-two-shoes best friend won't let me feel good about it. But she's right. And, now, I feel like a terrible person trying to convince myself that I did the right thing, and it's not working."

Raising his eyebrows, I nod subtly. "I see. Well, I can definitely try to help you with all of that. But we both will need your full participation to see progress, which will take time."

I understand that I need to be active in my own healing, which means being cognizant of old behaviors that I deemed normal for some time and rectifying them with new, healthier habits. Understanding this doesn't mean it's going to be easy.

Blithe is proud of me for taking the first step, and honestly, I cringed at the idea of sharing my shortcomings with a stranger, but I'm proud of myself, too. *Proud of what after a few sessions?* I'm not exactly sure, but I feel good knowing I will eventually be a better version of myself.

***

After the communication hiatus with Jamaal, we're happy to be regaining whatever we had before this big mess. He's now asking questions about the reason for the distance and I don't know if I can tell him. The whole reason for distancing myself from Jamaal was not to have anything or anyone thwart my plan against Xander. I didn't consider the feelings of anyone except my own. How do you tell someone you care about that you're a selfish human? Maybe tonight, I'll gather my courage during dinner at our favorite place.

I valet my car and walk through the entrance looking for the man who is fashionably early. Standing next to the Maître D, inhaling the delicious aroma's flooding the dining room, but suddenly remembering my last visit… with Xander. I quickly shrug it off so as not to taint the incredible memories Jamaal and I have created here.

The Maître D guides me to Jamaal, and I happily sit gazing at the delight on Jamaal's face.

Stretching his hand to mine. "I've been waiting for you to show up after all this time." He smiles.

I mirror his expression. "I can honestly say I've missed our time together, but there's something I feel like I need to share with you."

"Me first! I invited you here not only to see your face, but to ask you for exclusivity."

As he continues to hold my hand, my eyebrows raise abruptly, and my eyes feel like they could launch from their sockets.

"You and I have gone through stages of growth, and I can see that the mountain of bricks you once built, is beginning to crumble. I want to give us a chance to be happy together... Exclusively."

A montage of everything that could go wrong with this relationship fills my mind. The uncertainty of future happiness combined with the calamity of heartbreak, flows like a river as I struggle to exhale. I can feel the muscles in my face, now forcing the smile that was once effortless. I stare across the table through the guise of a smile as Jamaal's genuine elation shines through. *This* breaks me. The dam I've been desperately trying to use to hold back tears is collapsing. It feels like liters are escaping from my eyes.

"I'm so sorry, Jamaal. I'm broken. I can't give you what you want... I don't know how. There's a constant battle between my heart and my head of what I want versus what I need... And I just can't do this."

Jamaal raises his voice as I stand up from the well-manicured table to remove myself from any further embarrassment.

"So, you're just gonna walk away?! Just going to keep running from your problems?"

I quickly return to my seat, scanning the room for familiar faces. "I'm not running."

"Seems like that's ALL you've been doing, and like a dummy, I've chased you for a year. I LOVE you! You're not perfect. Neither am I. I saw your broken pieces, but I chose and still choose to see the full beauty you carry."

"You wouldn't say that if you knew what type of person I really am." Lowering my head.

"I don't think anything could hurt me as much as if you decide to walk away right now... Let. Me. In."

I'm fairly certain he's wrong. But I wipe my tears with the white handkerchief and readied myself to deliver the honesty Jamaal has been relentlessly trying to unearth. *You can do this*. I exhale heavily.

"I was engaged once to a man who required all of my love, and at the time, I thought was worthy of it. So, I happily gifted it to him. Then, he took my love *and* my ring to propose to another woman. I coincidentally witnessed it all. Talk about an imagine living rent-free in my mind."

"Franchesca, *that* doesn't make you a bad person."

"I know. I'm getting there. This man came back into my life, while I was casually dating you.

Xander tried to get back into my good graces, and for awhile I fought it but considered that this could be my chance to be happy again with the mature version of the 'one that got away.' So, when he proposed. I said yes."

"So, we both were pursuing you at the same time, and you chose him? Again. The man responsible for all the hoops I've had to jump through just to get close to you?"

I bury my face into my hands as his words slice into me like a freshly sharpened sword.

Forcing my words through the lump in my throat. "I know. I wasn't thinking of how you would feel. I'm sorry. I'm *so* sorry."

His once-pale face transitions from pink to red. The pain in my chest wants to stop here, but I've already come this far. I might as well rip his heart out. Quick and mercifully.

"Were you sleeping with him, too?" Jamaal inquires bitterly.

"No! Never. It was only you. But, I did leave him at the altar. He had been professing his love to me all this time, but he had a wife and child at home. So, I called her to witness the event. I was elated to destroy him. Everything he built, even his self-worth. And I didn't feel bad about it, until I was forced to resonate with how awful I was. *This* is why I can't do it. I don't deserve you, and you don't deserve me."

Jamaal attentively ingests all of my baggage, then aggressively hails our server for a bottle of Cabernet Sauvignon and the check.

"So, do you still want exclusivity with me?"

Part of me is hoping he will say yes, but only so I can feel like I'm not the most awful person on the planet, but I know better.

"I don't know." He nods. "I really don't know."

The server arrives with the bottle, and Jamaal places cash inside the billfold as he raises himself from his seat. Watching me intently, he approaches, and slowly leans in to kiss my forehead before making his way toward the exit. My body turns, and my eyes follow until he's out of sight. This moment made me realize that I am indeed in love with him.

But what do I do with it?

***

I can't stop thinking about Jamaal and yet I refuse to call like I'm some ego-driven teenage boy who is secretly afraid of rejection. Well, most of that is correct. But still. I don't want it to be.

I've been going to therapy for a couple months, and I'm working through my fears of commitment, among other things, and I'm grateful. One thing I've learned is no matter the relationship, it takes effort to maintain. Some are easier than others, but there's always the potential for disappointment and heartbreak, but how we decide to handle them dictates our recovery and healing. And he's helping me work on the 'how' so I don't miss out on opportunities for happiness by dwelling on the past.

Dr. Samuels seems to think inviting Jamaal to one of my sessions would be a good idea since his office is the only place, I openly express my feelings about him. I don't know what to think about it. It's terrifying. I can't bring myself to call him after all this time to just check in, let alone ask him to join my therapy session. *Is he crazy?*

After a few more weeks of encouragement, and kicking and screaming, I think I'm finally ready to allow myself to be vulnerable in a controlled environment.

Approaching Jamaal's front door, I release all the air in my lungs before I knock. Hoping with everything within me that he doesn't open the door. My knuckles tap the wood, and moments later he reveals his beautiful face for the first time in months. My eyes widen at the sight of his smile. *I miss that.*

"Franchesca?"

"Hi!" I reply breathlessly. "I'm sorry. You're probably busy. I just…"

Come on, Franchesca, when have you ever stumbled over your words? I swallow audibly before making a second attempt. "Umm, I've been going to therapy to sort out all my stuff and I talk about you. A lot. And my therapist thinks it would be a good idea for you to attend."

"And what do you think?"

"Oh. Me?" Jabbing my thumb into my chest. "Um, I think I agree with Dr. Samuels."

"I'll do anything to help support you on your journey." He winks.

Jamaal continues to stand in the doorway, and I, on the two-stair porch, gazing at each other. I stand there not knowing what to say, but also, not knowing how to leave, and he mirrors me effortlessly. Smiling blankly as if we can vividly see our shared memories through each other's eyes. It's a real-life daydream, until a car horn in the distance, snaps us back to reality.

"Okay. Well, I'll see you Friday at noon."

"You got it." He agrees.

On the drive, my hands clutch the steering wheel as if I'll never let it go. Wanting to be happy about revealing myself to Jamaal, but thoughts of uncertainty force my hands to squeeze even tighter. *Will he reject me? Is it too late? Will this all have been for nothing?*

"...Right?!" Jamaal finishes.

The inflection of his voice awakens me from my thoughts. "What?"

"Are you okay? I've been talking this entire time."

I nod as we pull into the lot of the doctor's office. Jamaal silently follows me up the stairs to Dr. Samuels's office. He welcomingly greets us and invites us up to get comfortable in his office.

"So, this is Jamaal. Nice to meet you." Dr. Samuels extends his hand. "Franchesca has something she would like to share with you, so we can start our session there."

Stunned by the expeditious nature of how Dr. Samuels decides to throw me into the hot seat, my eyes widen. I don't know how to start or exactly what to say. It will just be a flow of word vomit spewing craziness and confusion. My knee begins to shake as I try to find the words. I now hear the quiet in the room. It's deafening. Listening to adjustments as our bodies shift against the furniture, as they wait for me to pour the contents of my heart onto the floor. But then, I feel a soft embrace on my clenched fist resting on the sofa. I swiftly turn to him.

"I love you." Jamaal whispers.

My heart skips. Literally. Those three words feel like they mean more coming from him than they have from any other, and somehow, they give me the courage to gather myself. I turn the rest of my body toward him, and stare Jamaal in his loving eyes to offer him the truth. "I'm here to be a better version of the person I was. When we met, I thought you were great. I still think you are. And along the way I began to develop feelings for you that I hadn't felt in years. Feelings I never wanted to be hurt by again. So, I pretended I didn't have them and used you for what I was willing to accept from you. Sex and entertainment. I thought if I tried hard enough, I could push you out of my life, forget how I feel about you and move on. But you persisted and we got closer. I realized I didn't want you out of my life. I want everything you've been trying to offer me, I was just too afraid to accept it, but now, I think I'm ready to give it a real effort."

We all sit in silence for a moment, but this time, I bask in it. As I continue to stare upon Jamaal's face awaiting a response that wouldn't make me regret this entire session, he gleams with unbelievable elation. He pulls me into a bodily embrace that somehow releases all my anxiety. He continues to hold me, and I allow myself to melt in his arms. The fear and sadness slowly dissipate. I close my eyes and rest my head on his shoulder, wrapping my arms around him in a way he couldn't mistake. Holding him closer in an effort to liquify my emotions into his body. Genuinely expressing the unspoken love I have for him.

Unbreaking my own heart has been an arduous journey, but I'm happy I was coaxed into taking the first step. Taking the time to heal from my past was never something I thought I needed. But, after understanding how I allowed my trauma to fester, turning me rotten from the inside out, and seeing how it changed my outlook on relationships, it was the best thing I could've done for myself. The peace I feel from relinquishing the weight of building that brick wall, is... peaceful. It's the understanding that even on a sunny day, there's potential for rain and knowing you have the tools that will get you through the storm.

***

I've been in therapy for six months now, and I decided a few weeks ago that today would be my last day. Dr. Samuels has been a godsend in my life, and it's time for me to try to use what I've learned on my own. To celebrate, I invite Jamaal and Blithe over for a catered dinner. They've been the best support in my life through each ascending step, and I'd like to thank them properly. Readying myself as the caterer pours me a glass of white wine for the meal, I hear light taps at the door. *Sounds like Blithe's baby knocks.* Excitedly, I swing it open, almost spilling my wine. Both Blithe and Jamaal are standing before me. Running in place at the sight of them, with my arms spread, welcoming a group hug. In this moment, life seems to be putting its pieces where they belong.

"Oh my goodness, dinner smells delicious!" Blithe wafting the aroma toward her face.

"It's definitely not my cooking. It's from Petit Robert Bistro. You two are in for a French treat! Please sit down, sit down!" I point to the dining room table.

The caterer pours two more glasses of wine and Blithe wastes no time giving Jamaal the third degree. This is the first time they're meeting, but they are fully aware of one another. Although Blithe is 26, she has the soul of a 40-year-old mother. Always protective.

"So, Jamaal, any thoughts on how you'd feel if Xander came back around looking for round three?"

"Seriously?" I protest.

After a sip of wine, Jamaal removes himself from his seat and chuckles at the question. "Xander isn't a thought for me. But I do have one question."

He has our full attention as he strolls to my side of the table, retrieving something from his pocket. Fear immediately overwhelms my body as Blithe gasps beside me. I can't sit still long enough before he gets to me. I jolt from my chair looking around the room for logical escapes. He catches my eyes with his gaze as he stands inches in front of me. I have no choice except to offer a gaze in return. Jamaal gently grabs both my hands, and I open my mouth as my brain searches for the right words to say and not ruin the evening. He lifts his open palm, and inside lies an iridescent band trimmed in silver. I laugh hysterically at the amount of relief washing over me, and I turn to Blithe…

"IT'S A MOOD RING!" Continuing to cackle. "I love it!"

He slides the ring on my finger. "Will you be my girlfriend?"

I never thought I would be as happy as I was when things were good with Xander. I never thought I'd feel that emotion for anyone again, but Jamaal manages to seduce it from my soul effortlessly. To think I had been fighting him the entire time. I could've lost one of the best people I didn't know I had. In retrospect, it seems obviously neglectful and dumb on my part, but we can just add those to the list of characteristics I no longer want to posses.

"Of course, I'll be your girlfriend! Are you ready for a bumpy ride?" Offering a wink.

We all chuckle as the nervous laughter quickly tapers, then silence erupts as there's another knock at the door. We quickly turn to each other as if there's a possibility one of us invited an additional guest without notice.

"Don't worry, I'll grab it. You just enjoy that ring." Jamaal flirts as he walks toward the door.

Blithe and I begin a conversation until we hear a familiar voice.

"Who the hell are you?"

Blithe and I make a B-line for the door.

"I'm Jamaal. Franchesca's boyfriend. And you are?" Jamaal confidently states.

I turn to Blithe in disbelief. Stepping in front of Jamaal to take over the conversation. "What are you doing here, Xander?"

"Oh? Are you surprised to see me? You moved on so quickly, so I guess you won't need that ring you stole from me. Does your little boyfriend know that you're a runaway bride and a thief? I wouldn't marry *this* one if I were you, Ja-maal," Xander rages.

I could say so many things to Xander right now, but my desire to give him any emotional reaction that he could further use against me just isn't there.

"You would think you'd consider that engagement ring a parting gift for emotional damage, but apparently, you need it more than I do. Wait here."

I close the door leaving Xander in the hall while I retrieve the ring from my jewelry box. I was never sure what I would do with it, but returning it to Xander wasn't on the list. I thought maybe one day I'd randomly meet a guy and overhear how he needed a ring but couldn't afford it. I could be his fairy godmother of sorts. At least I'd know it would be in good hands. Honestly, I had forgotten I had it. It had been resting underneath all of my other preferred jewelry, but it is rightfully his, and I no longer have the desire to keep it.

Walking back to the door, flashing a grin in Jamaal's direction as I come face to face with Xander for what I hope will be the last time. I hold up the ring between my thumb and index fingers, and he snatches it from me.

"You ruined my life. I loved you. I risked everything for you."

"You did. You did risk everything. Your marriage, your friendships, and maybe even the respect of you daughter. But it wasn't for me. You did it for you. The only thing you didn't plan on was getting caught. You didn't love me. You loved the *idea* of me, and what having me meant for you. It's unfortunate you thought that was acceptable. I can't tell you how to live your life, but I can say that I dodged a very elusive bullet by walking away from you...Twice!" I chuckle. "You destroyed me emotionally. So, I thought I needed payback, and I sincerely apologize for the pain I caused. Hopefully, you can forgive me. I hope you learn from your mistakes, make better choices, and possibly heal from whatever it is that make you disregard women like you have."

Immediately closing the door as he yells about how terrible of a person I am, but somehow, I feel vindicated. I feel sorry for him, and I'm also sincerely sorry about what I did to him. But I owe him nothing. I allowed him to take parts of me I thought I'd never get back. I simply existed in my own life because someone I once adored hurt me. The power of forgiveness never rested in the hands of Xander, but I gave him so much control. I had to learn to forgive him without an apology. I had to make a choice. A choice I didn't know was an option four years ago. A choice that only healing could grant me the sight to see. That choice was me. And now that I'm recovering those pieces of myself, I want to gift them to the people in my life who truly deserve them.

APPENDIX A: Discussion Questions

Sometimes we struggle in relationships of all varieties, with family, friends and even ourselves. That struggle can lead to a downward spiral in behavior, perspective and how we choose to rationalize after toxicity has entered our lives. If we are uncertain on the proper ways to handle it, we will never learn that there are opportunities waiting for us to learn to love ourselves and others again, forgive and understand, but best of all, learn to heal. It's all about taking that first step.

Here are some discussion questions to get you started:

- How do you feel when someone has wronged you? Do you need time to forgive? Do you feel vengeful or choose to dismiss them from your life completely?
- When someone has wronged you, will you seek them out to understand their perspective through communication or try to push the feelings of hurt/anger away?
- What are some things that push your buttons? What situations happened in your life that allowed these things to become a trigger?
- Think about some events that have happened in your life that had a negative impact on your behavior or thinking long-term. Why do you think that impact lasted as long as it did?

165

Coming Soon

Like Podcasts? Me too! Just for you, I'll be hosting the Podcast "Let's Talk About It". We'll be sharing, understanding and discussing topics on how to give ourselves the love we need, setting personal boundaries, reconciliation, healthy vs. unhealthy relationships, healing and so much more!

To keep up with the Podcast, upcoming books and events, visit
tanaysawyer.com to sign up and stay in the know.

About the Author
(Dust cover flap: Back)

Tanay Sawyer is bringing the light at the end of a dark tunnel. Her life experiences of rediscovering the relationship with herself and learning how that translates into healthy relationships with others, introduced the desire to help those in similar situations. Through her novels in contemporary fiction and her voice in podcasting, she's helping people become better versions of themselves, create and sustain healthy relationships.

As an adult, she realized she suffered from traumas of her past. But instead of allowing trauma to continue having residence in her life and influence her future, she sought self-reflection, forgiveness and healing. Through her on-going journey, being a source of love and light became a priority.

Keep in touch at TanaySawyer.com

Dust cover flap: Front

Due to past trauma, Franchesca develops a fear of intimacy and vulnerability. To fill the void, she turns to sex for comfort and control, and begins to revel in it, to the point where she becomes unrecognizable. Unleashing her fury onto others, thinking she will be unscathed, before she reaches a crossroad forcing her to choose between what she wants most and what she needs.

Heartbreak is never easy.

It can ruin you if you let it.

Even when you think you've dodged a bullet.

Back Cover

After her fiancé fatally ripped her heart from her chest, just to sprinkle the confettied pieces at her feet. Franschesa thought it would be best to throw love to the wolves and grab lust by the hand.

Now, struggling with what has become an addiction, emotionally anorexic Franchesca uses her prowess as a sexual hypnotic for personal gain. But things begin to get hazy when her ex, Xander, returns to Boston to reclaim what was once his.

While Xander tries to sweep her off her feet, Franchesca has a plan of her own.